The Case of the Power Spell
A Hillcrest Witch Mystery
(Book #1)

Amorette Anderson

Copyright © 2018 All Rights Reserved

All rights reserved. No part of this publication may be reproduced, distributed, or transmitted in any form or by any means, including photocopying, recording, or other electronic or mechanical methods, without the prior written permission of the publisher, except in the case of brief quotations embodied in critical reviews and certain other noncommercial uses permitted by copyright law.

Table of Contents

Chapter One	5
Chapter Two	14
Chapter Three	22
Chapter Four	40
Chapter Five	50
Chapter Six	59
Chapter Seven	74
Chapter Eight	87
Chapter Nine	94
Chapter Ten	114
Chapter Eleven	125
Chapter Twelve	136
Chapter Thirteen	143
Chapter Fourteen	153
Chapter Fifteen	170
Chapter Sixteen	182
Chapter Seventeen	189

Chapter One

I place the skeins of yarn on my desk, lined up next to the sweater pattern in a little row; blue, yellow, grey.

Then I step back and look at the arrangement, imagining an Icelandic sweater with a blue and yellow decorative pattern around the neck, and grey body.

Hmm... Nope.

It's not quite right.

I rearrange the yarn; grey, blue, yellow.

Again, I visualize the sweater. No! This is all wrong. Too much yellow in the body.

Maybe I need to go back to the yarn store... For the *third* time today.

To say my PI business is slow these days is an understatement.

As I'm about to stuff the yarn back into the plastic shopping bag, I hear a knock at the door.

Maybe it's Marley, my best friend, here with an iced Americano.

Or maybe it's Sherry O'Neil, owner of the Nugget building in which my office is located, asking for rent.

It *is* the first of the month.

The knock sounds again. The rap-rap of knuckles on wood is too sharp to be Marley. Too demanding. It's got to be Sherry.

Drat.

I open the door slowly, my mind whirring as to how I might buy some time before paying her the three hundred that I'll owe for September. It's not much, but then, my office isn't much, either. It's a yoga studio storage closet actually, but I try hard not to think about that.

"Hi, Penny Banks?" The Mayor of Hillcrest, a tall, white haired man in his mid - sixties, is standing before me.

"Oh! Mayor Haywater," I say, opening the door wider. It's not Sherry! Inside, I'm doing a little victory jig. "What are you doing here?" I ask. Because, let's face it, the guy must be lost or something. Surely, he's not here to see *me*.

"Please, call me Cliff," he says. He extends his hand.

I shake it, still wondering how he's managed to get so lost that he ended up on the forgotten second floor of the Nugget building.

"I heard you have some sort of Private Detective operation going on here," he says, peering past me and into the room.

He's dressed in a white button up shirt that's tucked into his jeans. A worn, brown leather belt and sneakers top off the business-casual look. As he speaks, he's reaching into his shirt pocket, fidgeting with a folded piece of paper. He keeps half pulling it out and then stuffing it back in.

Maybe he *is* here to see me.

"Yes," I say. I step in, and motion to the wall above my desk, where my PI certificate is displayed. I found an ornate gold frame at Bess' Antique Haven. Inside of it, the certificate that was emailed to me after I completed a six-month online PI program looks very classy, if I do say so myself.

I make a gesture, à la Vanna White, as I say, "I'm certified, and I've been practicing for five years."

"I see," says Cliff, nodding. He stops fidgeting with the paper in his pocket, and now he's looking around the little space, as if he's uncertain of what to do next.

"Please, have a seat," I say, pulling my only chair forward.

It's important to exude professionalism when first greeting a client, according to class number one of my program. "To what end may I assist you?" I ask, rounding my desk and perching on my giant inflated Swiss Ball. For added effect, I place my hands into a 'power triangle', as my personal development guru, Jumper Strongheart suggests. With my fingers forming a tent, I give Cliff what I hope is a friendly, helpful, professional smile.

"To what end...?" he repeats. "Sorry, I don't understand your question."

Hm. It did come out sounding a bit vague. "I *meant*, how can I help you?" I say.

"Oh. Good. Yes... so you are taking on work at the moment?" He eyes my desk. "You look like you might have your hands full with... *other* work?"

I wish I'd had time to put away the yarn. And the knitting pattern. And the knitting needles. And the page full of doodles of my cat. And the half a dozen dirty mugs and one half-eaten bagel.

I've been meaning to clean all of this up, but when you sit alone all day in a supply closet -- er, I mean office -- you start to lose motivation for tidying.

I quickly start cleaning up the space, tossing the yarns on the floor at my feet.

As I work, I'm talking quickly. "No, no. This is just some silly knitting project." It almost kills me to call knitting silly, because it's not. It's a way of life.

"I wasn't even really working on it," I say. "I've got a few other cases going --" Can drawing doodles of my cat be called a case? Sure; The Case of the Cat Doodle. "--But I'm sure I can carve out some time in my schedule."

I finish clearing away the knitting needles and pattern, and then fish around for a spare piece of paper. Finding none, I flip my page of cat doodles over, and breathe a sigh of relief when I find the other side of the page blank.

"Just let me get prepared to jot down some notes," I mutter, hoping that I sound like I take on new cases all the time.

I fish around for a pen or pencil. My top desk drawer is crowded with bulk containers of gum (I like to chew while I knit), a box of feminine supplies (because inevitably, that time of the month arrives) and a cluster of tangled yarn (because, yes, that happened, and I got frustrated and stuffed the whole mess into the drawer. Out of sight, out of mind, as they say).

Not one pen.

Ah ha! A mechanical pencil! I pick it up and click the end, desperately hoping that there's some lead in it. No luck. I chuck it over my shoulder.

Cliff is watching me, a concerned look on his face. "Maybe I should come back at a better time," he says, carefully.

I don't have to be a graduate of 'Speedy's Online Private Investigator Licensure Program' to detect that Cliff Haywater was losing confidence in me. Fast.

He starts to stand up, looking at the door.

"Sit!" I say, sounding desperate. Probably because I *am* desperate. The knocking wasn't Sherry *this* time, but the next time, it will be.

I push my glasses up on my nose and take a deep breath. My eyes spot a pen. Thank goodness. I pick it up, and immediately feel better. I'm ready.

I square my shoulders and say, "Cliff, I'm a detective. I can help you with whatever issue you need investigated. I'm the only PI in town."

He's half sitting, half standing. He looks at me. I position the pen over the paper, ready to take notes -- as any organized, intelligent PI would do. "So, what's going on?" I ask.

He sits.

I breathe out a second sigh of relief.

He fishes in his pocket, and pulls out a piece of paper. "I found this," he says. "In my home recycling bin. I was looking for a receipt I'd thrown out. I can't figure it out…"

I jot down, *'looking for a receipt'* on my paper, just to look engaged.

He pushes the paper across the desk, towards me.

I pick it up and read it.

Express Travel Confirmation and Receipt for:
Melanie Haywater
Destination: Oahu, Hawaii
Flight information:
Departure: Flight A1665 Departing Denver at 3:05 pm on August 15, 2018

You have no return flight booked for this trip.

Melanie, your flight is confirmed! Your confirmation number is 73010188
Please be sure to check in online at expresstravel.com for boarding prior to your trip.

I look up at Cliff. "What's so confusing about this?" I ask. "It looks like your wife, Melanie, booked a one-way trip to Hawaii on August fifteenth. That was, what… two weeks ago?" I try to do the math in my head. It's the first of September. *Thirty days, hath September, April, May, and November…*

I wish I had a calendar available. I make a note to bring one in.

"Did she go?" I ask.

Cliff shakes his head.

"That's the odd thing about all this," he says. "I can't figure it out. She hasn't gone anywhere. But I checked our bank account, and I see the charge for the ticket. Why did she buy it, and then not use it?"

"Did you ask her?" I ask.

He nods. His face becomes a little bit flushed. We're getting into uncomfortable territory here, I can tell.

"I did," he says, stiffly. He's quiet for a moment, as if thinking. Then he sits up straight, and clears his throat. "She wouldn't tell me," he says. "She refused to talk about it, actually. Which is why I thought of you. I was hoping you might do some digging, maybe call this 'Express Travel' place and see when the tickets were booked, or talk to her sister, Gale. She tells Gale everything."

"Hm," I say. I'm not so sure about this. Why should I go snooping around in my Mayor's marriage? I'm getting the impression that's it's not exactly a healthy relationship, if she's hiding something like a one-way ticket. This feels like a can of worms better left lidded.

"I'll pay you well," Cliff says, removing his wallet from his back pocket. He takes out a crisp hundred-dollar bill, and places it on my desk. Then, a second.

I'm warming up to the idea.

He continues. "This is really important to me. If my wife wants to travel to Hawaii, I'd like to take her there. Maybe I could get us *both* tickets, as a surprise. It could be good for us."

He thumbs through his bills, and then, to my delight, he takes out a third hundred. "Will you see what you can dig up?" He asks me, pushing the little stack forward.

Considering I have zero dollars saved up for the rent that is due today, I nod my head. I can't say no to this.

Besides, maybe Cliff is right.

Maybe, by uncovering the truth, I could *save* the Haywater's marriage. Cliff could purchase two round trip tickets to Hawaii, and the happy couple would thank me for my help, for years to come.

A sinking feeling in the pit of my stomach tells me that won't be the case, but I do my best to ignore it as I pick up the bills. "I will start today," I say.

"Well, now, don't ignore your other cases, just for this," Cliff says, standing up. "You can get to it when you get to it.".

"Oh, it's no problem," I say. "My other work is of a long-term variety." The Case of the Cat Doodles will go on for years, I'm guessing. "This will take precedence," I say.

"Thank you." Cliff gives a business-like nod, and then reaches into his wallet again. This time, he pulls out a business card. "I'm always around town, and I'm sure you know where my offices are." He hands the card to me. "When I'm not at my offices, I'm at The Other Place," he says.

In addition to being Hillcrest's mayor, Cliff Haywater also owns The Other Place (or The OP, as us locals call it), which is a local watering hole on main street. He also used to own The Place, which is practically Hillcrest's only restaurant. However, I recall now that a few weeks back, he'd sold it.

"That's right," I say. "You're not running The Place any more. How do you like semi-retirement?"

Cliff grunts. "Oh, I'd hardly call it semi-retirement. I'm still busy as always with The OP and my duties as mayor. I thought selling the restaurant would give me more time on the golf course," he shakes his head and emits a polite chuckle. "No such luck. Now I just end up spending more hours fussing over town politics in my office or working at the bar." He points to the card that is now in my hand. "But if you can't find me at either of those two places, just give my cell phone a call."

I look down at the card as I stand and walk towards the door. "Will do," I say. I open the door for him, and he's about to step out, when something stops him. I don't like the uncomfortable look on his face. I sense that he's about to say something he really doesn't want to say.

"There's one more thing," he says.

"What's that?" I ask.

"Melanie... Melanie's been crying a lot lately. I don't know if that's of any relevance, but... you should probably know."

Great.

Any sliver of hope that this is all going to end happily is fading quickly. "Okay," I say carefully. "Thanks for the information. When did that start?"

"Well, it was after the fiasco with the deep freezer at The Place."

I'd heard about that. The Place's head chef, Joe Gallant, was found dead in the restaurant's walk-in freezer. It seemed that he'd gotten stuck inside and froze to death. The freezer, usually set at thirty degrees Fahrenheit, had been found at negative two.

"It was a terrible accident," Cliff goes on. "On the *last* day that I was the owner, no less. August fourteenth. Not the best way to go out..." He shakes his head. "Terrible luck. I can't quite understand it. That freezer never gave me one issue, in all those years, and then to have it act up on the very last day."

"That is unfortunate," I agree.

"And Melanie was there, you know, when he was found," Cliff says. "At first, I thought she was crying because it was such a traumatic event. It really was, too. He was blue and had icicles growing out of his nose. But it's been two weeks, I thought it would pass, but she's still crying constantly. I'm beginning to think it's not about the dead body at all. I'm starting to wonder, since finding this ticket, if her being upset has something to do with Hawaii.... Though I can't fathom what."

I frown. "I'll look into it," I say. "That's very helpful."

He nods. "Good. I thought it might be." He seems very relieved to have that bit of the conversation over with. "Well, then! I guess that's it. We'll be in touch!"

"I'll reach out with an update in the next few days," I promise, as Cliff heads for the stairs.

Chapter Two

Back in my office, I stare at the sheet of paper that Cliff handed me, detailing Melanie's travel plans.

A one-way ticket to Hawaii. Constant crying. *Hm.*

Even without doing one lick of investigating, I've started forming conclusions about the case.

Melanie clearly isn't happy in her marriage; not talking to her husband, secretly booked tickets, and chronic crying jags do not equal a happy wife.

My shoulders slump.

I do *not* want to be the one to tell Cliff that his wife is not happy.

After a few minutes of dwelling on this, a phrase from Jumper Strongheart, my personal development guru, comes to mind: *Are you a worrier, or a warrior?* I can imagine him pacing the stage, asking the audience this question. I've never seen him live, but I'd love to. I imagine him in my little office, pacing back and forth and speaking into a headset. '*Are you a worrier, Penny Banks, or a warrior?*' he'd ask.

"Warrior!" I say out loud

The sound of my own voice jolts me, and I start tipping backwards on my Swiss Ball. Then I fall backwards off the exercise ball, and land with a thud on the floor, my dress up around my waist. I am so glad *that* didn't happen when Mayor Haywater was in the room.

I silently curse Jumper Strongheart and his *'Strong Spine -- Strong Life'* protocol, which forbids chair-sitting.

I prop myself up onto my elbows. My feet are still high up on the ball. From down here, I can see the yarn that I tossed onto the floor, along with the empty mechanical pencil. It reminds me of how pitifully I handled the 'intake' of my new client.

I am cringing as I struggle to my feet. On the blank piece of paper, I jot down a few notes to myself, so that I can learn from the situation.

> 1. *Improve my client intake skills. How to look more professional? Clean desk! Plant in the office?*
> 2. *Work on core stability. Sit-ups every morning? Reread Jumper's strong spine protocol. Must be able to balance on ball!*
> 3. *Don't take husband-wife cases. Too sad!*

There. I think that about covers it. I think I'm about done for the day. I'll tackle this again in the morning, when I feel fresh.

Though it's been a rough day -- a *learning experience*, as Jumper would call it -- there is one good thing that happened. I have three hundred dollars! I can pay my rent.

I happily stuff the cash into my wallet, and then go about emptying coffee mugs.

The supply closet has one little window, which opens and doesn't have a screen. When I poke my head out of it, I can see down to the sidewalk below. I pour mug after mug of stale coffee and tea out onto the empty sidewalk, where there's always a brown stain in between rain storms (thanks to me).

Once this is done, I stuff three of the empty mugs, into my cross-body messenger bag. Then I carefully don my bag and head for the door.

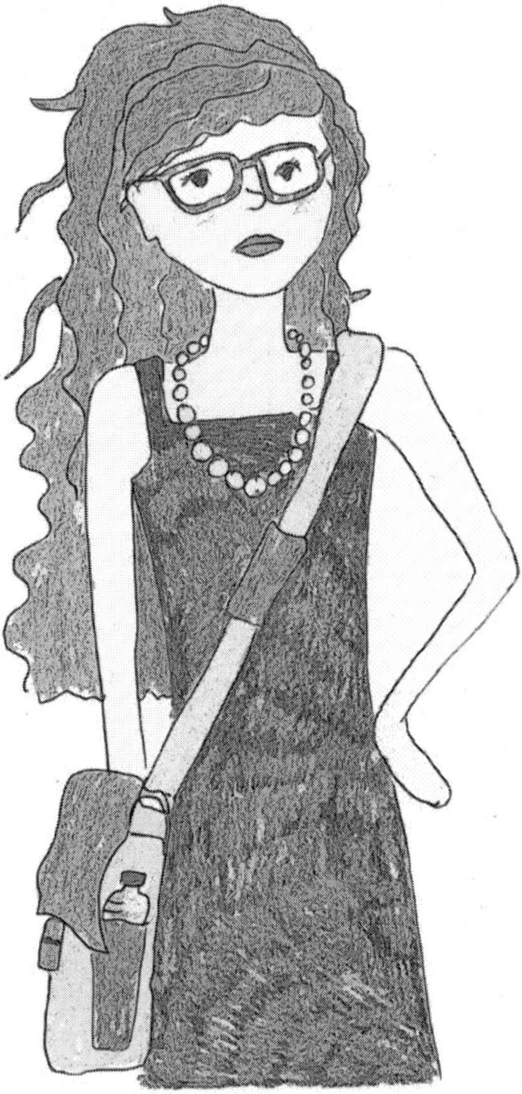

Soon I'm at home, scrubbing coffee stains out of mugs. I'm elbow deep in suds when I hear a knock on the door.

I have a feeling it's Chris, and I'm right.

When I open the door, he's standing there. He immediately leans in and gives me a kiss on the cheek.

I'm wearing bright yellow rubber dishwashing gloves that are dripping with soap suds, so I don't wrap my arms around his neck like I want to. Instead I grin and accept the kiss.

Chris Wagner is my boyfriend. He's also a police captain for the Hillcrest Police Department. It's a small department of four, and he's a star player.

It's a position he's good at.

In fact, when I first developed a crush on Christopher Wagner, he was the captain of the Hillcrest High School Boys Basketball team. I was a girl four years younger than him, drooling from the bleachers. All these years later, he's still handsome as heck, and I'm still his biggest fan.

Chris is tall and in great shape, with blue-grey eyes and sandy blonde hair. Tonight, he's dressed in basketball shorts and a black tee shirt. Best of all, he has a six pack of beer in one hand, and a pizza in the other.

"Hungry?" he asks, as I reach for the pizza.

"Starving!" I say. "I was about to pour a bowl of cereal. This is so much better!"

Chris laughs. As he enters the apartment, I smell his body wash. I see now that his hair is also still a bit wet, like he just stepped out of the shower. I know what that means.

"Did you just get home from work?" I ask.

Chris has two looks: either he's dressed in his police uniform, or he's just peeled it off, and is unwinding so that he can perform well in his next shift. His life is totally centered around his work. He loves being a police officer.

I don't blame him. I wanted to be one, too. I went to college for my criminal justice degree, and then entered Hillcrest's police academy immediately after. That's actually when Chris and I first hooked up. He was the trainer of my academy class. We kissed on day one, and in the days that followed, we did more than kiss.

A *lot* more.

Looking back now, I see what a mistake it was. I should have ignored my feelings for Chris, and tried to get through the academy without bedding my instructor. Maybe then, Academy would have gone better for me. As it was, I was an emotional mess, and I failed out of it. Not long after that, Chris and I broke up.

Needless to say, I thought my life was over.

I had to say goodbye to my dream career and my dream guy, all within one week. I was crushed.

However, the saying is true: Every dark cloud *does* have a silver lining.

In the months and years after I hit rock bottom, I found Zumba, knitting, and my PI program. And look at me now! I'm running my own not-so-successful PI business, and almost-knitting an Icelandic sweater! Plus, Chris and I got back together -- sort of -- a few months back. We're taking it slow; maybe things aren't as passionate as they were the first time around, but we've gotten into a comfortable sort of groove. Does it get any better than that?

You don't really have to answer that.

With a hissing sound, Chris cracks open a beer and hands it to me.

"Thanks," I say, accepting it. "How was work? Did you just get off?"

He nods, and then opens a beer for himself and takes a swig. "Twenty minutes ago," he says. He opens the pizza box and a cloud of steam billows upwards.

"That was fast," I say, trying to calculate in my head how in the world Chris managed to ride his mountain bike home from the police station, pick up cold beers, order a pizza, take a shower, and make it over to my place (which is right next door) in twenty minutes. Sometimes it takes me that long just to wash my hair.

I do have really long, thick hair, while Chris's is only slightly longer than a buzz cut, but still.

"I'm getting the routine, down," Chris says, grinning as he pulls a slice of the pie towards him. A long string of cheese stretches out from the slice, and he has to sever it with his fingers.

"I ordered the pizza before I jumped in the shower," he explains. "Plus, I started getting a few six packs each time I'm at the store, so that I don't have to run out every time."

"You're a wise man," I say, reaching for a slice myself.

Chris laughs. "How was your day?" he asks.

"Good," I say. Then, before I think too much about it, I say, "Mayor Haywater visited me, at my office."

"Was he lost?" Chris asks.

I glare at him, while chewing my pizza. Yes, I thought the same thing, but that doesn't mean *he* can think it.

"No," I say, once I swallow the pizza and wash it down with beer. "You really have no respect for my PI career, do you? He wanted to see me. He wants me to spy on his wife," I say. "She ordered a one-way ticket to Hawaii, but never went. He's worried."

Chris gulps down some beer. Then, after a minute of thought he says, "Be careful with that, Penny. It sounds messy. He might *think* he wants to know what's going on with Melanie, but I doubt he's going to be happy when you present him with the facts. People tend to shoot the messenger."

"I know." My shoulders slump. "It's not good. But he offered cash, and I couldn't pass it up."

We eat in silence for a bit. Turkey, my calico cat, joins us and I toss him occasional bits of cheese, which he scoops up with his tongue while his tail twitches happily.

As I eat, I'm thinking about my conversation with Cliff. "Hey, Chris," I say. "Remember how Joe Gallant was found in the walk-in freezer, at The Place?"

"How could I forget?" Chris asks. He stops eating. "It was horrible." He places his piece of pizza down on the box top, which reminds me that I didn't get out plates for us.

I hop off of my barstool and round the counter to grab some plates.

The cupboards are empty. Did I forget to run the dishwasher again?

I reach for paper napkins instead, and push a few over towards Chris. Then, I search the cupboards for glasses. I find one clean recycled mason jar, and one juice glass. I fill each with water and carry them back towards my stool. I've learned long ago that if I'm going to drink beer up here in the mountains, I need to drink water along with it.

"How did he get stuck in there?" I ask.

Chris shrugs. "It was an old freezer. The handle from the inside jammed, and the thermostat was all screwy as well. When we got there, the thing was at negative two. My chief thinks, that's what made the handle jam -- maybe the lower temperature froze the release mechanism."

"Why did the temperature go down so low?" I ask.

"Who knows?" Chris says. "Old machines malfunction all the time. It's hard to say."

"What if someone *turned* it down," I say.

Chris shoots me a warning look. "Penny, don't go imagining things," he says. "We checked out the security footage, from The Place. No one out of the ordinary went in or out of the restaurant."

"Who did, then?" I ask.

Chris looks reluctant to tell me, so I ask again. "Come on, Chris, you can tell me. Who went into the restaurant that day?" I ask.

He's still thinking.

I ask a third time.

I think that there's a reason for that saying, 'the third time's the charm,' because this time he answers me.

"Let's see..." he says, looking up and to one side as he recalls the footage. "Joe went into the kitchen first, around ten A.M. Then there was Ralph, Cliff's assistant, at about eleven. Then, Glenn, the assistant cook. He was in and out a few times. After that, Cliff, at about two thirty. Last, there was Melanie. She went in at around three. That was it. The medics and police were called in at about three thirty, when the body was discovered."

"Did the medics say how long he'd been dead for?" I ask.

He shakes his head. "They couldn't determine that, without performing an autopsy. We didn't think that was necessary."

"Chris... what if....? What if one of those people *murdered* Joe Gallant, and made it *look* like an accident? And what if that's connected, somehow, to Melanie's one-way ticket?"

"How could the death of Joe be connected to Melanie's trip to Hawaii?" Chris asks.

"I don't know," I say. But I'm going to find out.

Chapter Three

When I wake up the next morning, I have a slight headache. It turns out, drinking three beers *can't* be mitigated with one eight-ounce glass of water.

Sure, Chris and I had fun playing our favorite card game and listening to O.A.R. until eleven P.M., but was it worth this hangover?

I smile to myself, remembering how good it felt to laugh with him, and then kiss on the couch with playing cards scattered all around us.

Yep. Definitely worth it.

I shower, dress in all black (a habit of mine these days), and then make my way to the kitchen to put on a pot of coffee. Turkey, already up, is sitting on a barstool, peering over the edge of the countertop to a Hillcrest Crier that is spread out before him.

"You would look so cute with a pair of reading glasses on," I say telepathically to Turkey, as I walk up to him and petting him on the top of the head.

That's right… I can talk to my cat, inside my head.

I'm not imagining things.

It's real.

He shakes off my affection. "I don't need reading glasses," he responds.

"Neither do I," I transmit. "But I wear them, because Jumper Strongheart says you can --"

"Wear an accessory to help you feel like the person you want to become. I know, I know. Fake it 'til you make it. You've told me a thousand times."

"Sheesh," I say, rummaging through the fridge in search of some orange juice. "*Someone's* in a bad mood."

"Well, that's what happens when I have to listen to loud music that hasn't been popular since 2004, until almost midnight," Turkey grumbles.

"Oh, don't be dramatic. Chris left at eleven," I say.

"Still," my cat transmits. "It was late. And that music is awful. Every song sounds the same."

"I love O.A.R.!" I protest. I haven't found any orange juice, so I settled on tap water. It's less than refreshing, but I make myself gulp it down. The coffee sizzles into the pot, and smells delicious.

I ready a travel mug, and then look for creamer in the fridge. Again, I come up empty handed. Black it is.

I really need to go grocery shopping.

"You're seriously telling me you don't like O.A.R.?" I ask. I swear, sometimes I think my cat and I got along better *before* I learned telepathy.

I picked up the skill about three months ago, when I started practicing witchcraft.

Let me back up a bit.

This past July, an elderly woman named Claudine Terra died. In a roundabout way, I inherited a book from her, called '*The Art and Science of Becoming a Witch*, or ASBW, as I like to call it.

All of a sudden, after reading the book, I had all kinds of magical abilities. I learned how to perform the Love Spell, and I started talking to my cat. I even pulled off levitating once, though I haven't been able to do it since.

I also shared the book with my knitting group. All the ladies loved it. We've been studying it every Wednesday night, for the past three months, though we haven't gotten super far. In fact, out of thirteen cycles (which are pretty much like chapters), we're still on cycle one.

Anyhow, now that I can communicate with Turkey, I'm finding out all these things about him that honestly, I'd rather not know.

Case in point? His dislike of O.A.R. -- one of my favorite bands.

Don't get me wrong. I love my cat. I'd do anything for him. It's just that -- If I'm being honest -- it was easier being his roommate before all these words were exchanged between us.

Back then, we communicated with pats on the head and kisses on the nose.

"Turkey, remember when you were a kitten?" I say, smiling as I think back to those simpler times. "You used to curl up in my palms. You were this big!" I hold my hands up, showing him his size.

"Why do you insist on calling me Turkey?" he asks. "You know I prefer Thomas Edison Fullbright."

I pour hot coffee into my mug. "You're always going to be Turkey to me," I say, as I carry my travel mug towards the living room. When I pass by Turkey, I lean down and give him a kiss on the top of the head. This time, he doesn't shake it off. Progress.

"It's too hard of a habit to break. You know I tried…" I scan the living room. "Have you seen ASBW? I have knitting circle tonight."

"Yes..." Turkey gracefully leaps off his stool and struts over towards the couch. He paws at the thin, hardbound ASBW, which is jammed between two couch cushions.

"I was reading the section on familiars yesterday, while you were out," he says, while he bats at the book's spine. "It started falling into the cracks. I couldn't get it out. Everytime I tried, it just went further in."

"Oh, you poor thing," I say sincerely. I've honestly never felt more grateful for my opposable thumbs than when I talk to Turkey. He points out so many inconveniences of having paws.

I pull the book from between the cushions, and stuff it into my bag. Then I head for the door. I wish I could take Turkey out with me, but since I know it's going to be a long and busy day, I think he will be more comfortable at home, where he can nap.

"Have a good day!" I call out, before he can say anything else negative, to bring down my mood.

It's essential that I stay positive this morning.

I have to approach this investigation into Melanie's unfulfilled travel plans with an open, optimistic outlook, if I hope to make any progress at all.

I stuff my closed coffee mug into my bag and get on my bike. As I start to pedal, my thoughts kick into a higher gear. I swear, I do some of my best detective work while I ride my bike. Once, I was riding to work, when I realized who was stealing Payday candy bars from the Hillcrest Market.

You might not think it to be an issue, but for a little store with a very narrow profit margin, the loss of fifty candy bars a month was surprisingly harmful to their bottom line.

I make it to my office without having one brilliant idea. Not one.

The day takes another turn for the worst when I spot a figure, walking down the street towards me. He is all too familiar.

I feel my heart beginning to pound, and my palms begin to sweat.

Doctor Maxwell Shire.

I met Max this past July, around the same time that I inherited ASBW. It wasn't a mere coincidence. Max actually came to town, specifically looking to buy the book from me. Apparently, it's very rare and valuable. I didn't give up the copy, but I don't think Max ever gave up trying to get his hands on it. Or me.

There's that, too. He seems to have a bit of a thing for me.

I have to admit, I kind of have a thing for him, too. I mean, I *am* with Chris, but I can't help it if I find this guy attractive, can I?

Oh, and did I mention he's a vampire!?

"Penny!" Max calls out. "Penny Banks. It's so good to see you!"

"You too," I say, blushing profusely as he approaches.

I get off my bike, careful not to flash too much leg, and then lock it up along with the others in a rack outside. Max lingers around me as I fumble with my bike lock.

When he stands close to me like this, my fine motor skills get all out of whack. I've learned that it has something to do with vampires' high testosterone levels, given all the wild game they consume. It reacts with the high estrogen levels of witches, or something like that. I don't exactly have the science down. All I know is that the man *affects* me.

Finally, I'm able to lock my bike. As I straighten up, he's staring at me, grinning. He is well aware of the effect he has on me, and he always seems to enjoy it.

His dark eyes sparkle. His black hair is longer than I remember, and his tan is deeper. He's wearing tight fitting shorts that stop just above his knee, and a tank top that reads 'Namaste'. I spot a yoga mat strapped to his back.

"It's been a while," I say, trying to sound casual. In fact, it's been two months, one week, and four days since I last saw Max Shire. Not that I'm counting or anything. "What brings you to town? Besides yoga…?"

We start walking up the steps together.

"I was hired at the college," Max says.

I stop walking. "*Hillcrest* College?" I ask. "I thought you lived far, far away from here."

"I *did* live far, far away from here," he says. "But now I live very, very close by."

He's standing very close to me. I can feel that testosterone-estrogen thing happening. It feels kind of sizzlely and tingly. I'm not sure if it's healthy.

I take a step back.

"Are you teaching... er... vampire classes?" I ask.

One of Max's passions in life is to teach others how to become Vampires. Not the human-blood-sucking kind. Max only advocates animalitarianism, meaning he sticks to sucking the blood of wild animals. It still strikes me as barbaric, but at least it's not life threatening.

"Not exactly," he says. "I'm starting out in Anatomy and Physiology. It's a good foundation, but not specific enough to scare anyone off. We'll see where it goes from there."

"Great," I say. "So do you plan on staying... for a long time?"

"Many, many years," he says. "As long as it takes," he adds.

I swallow. What's *that* supposed to mean? "Then I guess I'll be seeing more of you," I say.

"*Much* more of me," Max says, with a sly grin. He motions towards the yoga studio door. "Are you going in for the Vinyasa Flow?"

"No," I say, shaking my head.

"You don't do yoga?" he asks, a look of concern clouding his handsome features.

"Not really," I say. "I'm more of once-a-week Zumba kind of a girl."

"Oh, Penny, you really should start up a yoga practice," he says. "Humans tend to have incredibly tight muscles, ligaments, and tendons. All of that shortening can

28

really throw off the body's alignment. Poor alignment can lead to all kinds of long term, chronic deficits."

"I'll take a look at the schedule," I promise.

"You might want to start with a nice, gentle Yin class," Max suggests. "I know how *tightly wound up* you tend to be."

He looks me over, in that way he does, from head to toe. Do vampires have x-ray vision or something? Because I feel like Max is looking straight through me.

It makes me feel light headed.

"I work just upstairs," I mumble, backing up. "I've gotta go."

I back up more, until my heels hit the wooden staircase that leads up to my office. He watches me, as I almost fall. Still blushing, I turn and start running up the stairs.

I'm breathing hard by the time I make it inside and slam the door behind me. The more barriers between Max and I, the better.

It takes me a whole hour of knitting to calm down. Since I haven't started my sweater project yet, I take on a couple of dozen rows to a scarf I've been working on for ages. The repetitive movements soothe me. Once I feel my pulse rate return to normal, and the heat in my cheeks dissipates, I pick up my pen.

I start writing notes right below where I left off, the day before.

This time, I'm writing a list.

Joe Gallant: Murder Suspects

1. *Ralph*
2. *Glenn*
3. *Cliff*
4. *Melanie*

I stare at the list for a minute. Then, without a clear plan in mind, I fold up the piece of paper. I've got to start somewhere, and Melanie makes sense. She's the one who's been mysteriously weeping, and who booked a one-way flight to Hawaii, yet never went.

I want to know why.

She might also be an easy person to find, because I know that she doesn't work. Usually, she can be found puttering around in the garden of the Haywaters' front yard. An added bonus is that the Haywaters live just next door to my friend Annie's cafe.

My coffee from home is long gone, and I'm craving an iced Americano with soy.

With that in mind, I head off to track down Melanie.

After a quick stop at the cafe to fill my travel mug, I reach the Haywaters' house. As suspected, Melanie is out front, on her knees in front of a rose bush. I lean my bike against the white picket fence, and walk towards the front gate.

"Hi... Melanie?" I say, as I reach the gate.

She stands up. It's eleven in the morning. The September sun is higher in the sky, and it's right in her eyes. She holds a garden-gloved hand to her brow and squints at me.

"Hi," I repeat. "I'm Penny Banks. I'm a private investigator in town. Mind if I come in?"

"I know who you are," Melanie says. "What's this about?"

She hasn't smiled yet. In fact, as she squints at me, her expression is very sour.

I hope I look like Melanie when I reach my fifties. I mean, I know that she's fifty-four because there was a town-wide birthday party for her last year, at The Place, but she doesn't *look* a day over thirty-five. She's slender and pretty, with salon-styled shoulder length blonde hair, and perfectly done makeup, despite the fact that she's doing yard work.

"I was just hoping I could ask you a couple of questions," I say.

I can't tell her that her husband hired me, so I start improvising. "I'm verifying some facts about Joe Gallant's death," I say, which isn't far from the truth. "It would be helpful if I could run some things by you. I've heard you were at the restaurant that day."

A nervous look crosses her face. At the same time, she walks towards the gate. "Yes, come in."

When she unlatches the gate, she studies me. "I didn't know the police were still interested in that," she says. Her voice quivers.

She's definitely nervous.

"I'm not with the police," I clarify. "I work for myself."

"But someone hired you to look into Joe's death?" she asks.

Shoot. I wasn't prepared for that question! "Yes," I say, and then quickly follow up with, "I understand that you were at The Place on the day that Joe was Found? That was August fourteenth, wasn't it?"

She nods. She's still looking at me like she can't quite figure out what she thinks of me. I get the feeling that she doesn't really want to have this conversation, but that she also doesn't want to be seen standing out on her front lawn talking to me.

"Would you like some coffee?" she asks.

I already have full travel mug of iced americano in my bag, but I want to talk to Melanie so I agree.

We head up the walkway, and I take in the perfectly pruned rose bushes and blooming peonies as we go. Inside, her house is spotless, which makes me feel guilty about my own poor housekeeping skills. Melanie leads the way into the kitchen, and goes right to the coffee maker. She begins emptying out the old coffee, so that she can brew fresh. I stand awkwardly near the counter, not sure where to begin.

Finally, after searching my brain for something that would start off the conversation right, I blurt out, "It must have been awful, seeing Joe's body. I heard he had icicles hanging out of his nose. Did you have nightmares?"

She immediately turns pale, and then the spoon she's holding clatters to the countertop. She reaches for the edge of the counter to brace herself, and suddenly, she bursts out into tears.

Oops. That may not have been the most graceful way to start my interview.

But the ball's already rolling, so I continue. "He was already dead when he was found, is that correct?" I ask, while looking around the kitchen for a Kleenex. I'm not cold-hearted, just socially awkward at times. I want to comfort her.

Not finding any tissues, I reach for a roll of paper towels and tear off half of one. When I walk towards Melanie and hand it to her, she takes it with a shaking hand.

"Yes," she says, between sobs. "It was awful. He was -- oh! Poor Joe -- he was dead when Cliff found him. The medics didn't know how long he'd been dead for, but they said that it could have been hours."

"Tell me about that day," I say. "What was happening in the kitchen?"

With great effort, Melanie picks up the spoon that fell from her hands, and begins measuring the ground coffee from a little tupperware into the waiting coffee-maker. She's still crying but trying to function anyway. It's an interesting sight to watch. Her hostess instincts are overriding her emotional breakdown.

"Do you take cream and sugar?" she asks, and then she dabs at her eyes while trying to look at me.

"Sure," I say.

As she crosses the kitchen to get cream from the fridge, she begins talking. It seems easier for her to talk if she's doing something else at the same time. "Cliff and I had been at the park that afternoon," she says. "The town hosted that retirement party for him," she says. "Not that he was really *retiring* -- he still has The OP and his mayor responsibilities. But stepping away from The Place was a big deal for him."

"That's right." I remember hearing about the party. "From noon to two, right? Lunch was served?"

She nods. "A bunch of members of town council organized a potluck. Were you there?"

I'd missed the party, and I tell her so. "Was there a good turn-out?" I ask.

"Of course," Melanie said. "You know how this town idolizes Cliff." Her tone is bitter here, which interests me. I don't get a chance to dig into it though, because she continues. "Cliff knew that The Place would be packed that night, because it was his last night as the owner. Right after the party, Cliff went in to help Joe and Glenn with prep work."

"Did he do that often?" I ask. "I mean, work in the kitchen?"

Melanie nodded. "My husband is *constantly* working," she says. "Even if he doesn't have to, he'll go into The Place or The OP and bus tables or help out behind the bar. He's been a workaholic for as long as I can remember -- all thirty years of our marriage." She sighs heavily, and then turns towards a cupboard and reaches for two mugs.

"What happened next?" I ask. "After the party, Cliff headed off to work at the restaurant, getting ready for the rush he expected. What did you do?"

"I came home to freshen up," she says, avoiding my eye. "Then, I went in to the restaurant to.... to visit Cliff." These words are rushed, and as she speaks she wipes a dishcloth furiously back and forth over the counter, though the black granite is already polished and spotless.

She's hiding something from me.

"You didn't do anything else?" I ask. "You just came home and then went to the restaurant?"

She nods.

"What time did you arrive at The Place?" I ask.

"About three, I'd guess." She says. She finally stops polishing and looks at me. "When I got there, Cliff and Glenn were hard at work. You know, chopping and mixing and what not. They said that Joe didn't turn up for his shift."

She looks away from me, and reaches up again with the now damp, mascara stained paper towel I handed her to dab her eyes. Tears are starting to flow again.

As she turns, she catches sight of the coffee pot. It's filling nicely. As if she's eager to have something to do, she takes a few strides towards it.

Her back is to me as I say, "And what did you do, when you got there?"

Her back and shoulders jump up and down as she takes a few jagged breaths. I can tell she's trying to center herself but it's not really working.

I give her a minute.

When she turns around, she has the coffee pot in her hands. She walks over and fills our mugs. I'm a coffee hound, so I start doctoring mine up right away, and then take a few long slurps.

The pause in conversation allows Melanie to collect herself, and when she speaks again, it's in an even, metered tone.

"I wasn't there long," she says. "Cliff and Glenn were rushing around, so busy trying to get ready for a full house, you know. Cliff said something about needing to pull a box of mac and cheese from the freezer. He went over to the door, but he couldn't open it."

She presses her lips together. Her eyebrows tent. Her nostrils flare. She's giving a valiant effort to stay in control.

I slurp my coffee, waiting.

"Cliff had to pull on the door really, really hard. When it opened, he almost lost his balance. He walked in and started shouting for help. Glenn went over, and they started -- oh! It was so terrible -- they started dragging Joe out of the freezer." Her hand, covering her mouth, is shaking.

"I'm so sorry that you had to see that," I say. I really am. I've seen dead bodies before, and it is *not* a pleasant experience.

She nods.

I'm about to ask her to describe the body, but I think better of it. I already know that Joe was dead, blue, stiff, and icicle-ridden. Asking her to go into the nitty-gritty details would only upset her, more than she already is. See? I'm learning.

"Did the medics and police arrive, soon after?" I ask.

"Yes," she says. "Cliff called out to me, and asked me to call nine-one-one. I was... well, I was in shock, really. It was difficult to dial the phone. The rest feels like a dream --" Her eyes go vacant as she recalls the way the afternoon progressed. "The paramedics pronounced him dead. The police asked us a few questions. Then, the restaurant started to fill up. Cliff and Glenn had to go about serving dinner. Of course, nothing was served from the freezer."

"That's good," I say.

Melanie continues. "I couldn't stay. How they went on as if nothing had happened is beyond me. That's Cliff. All business. Once he has an idea in mind, he'll stick to it no matter what happens. He'd planned on announcing who he would sell the restaurant to that very evening. I couldn't take it. I came home, and went to bed early."

"I don't blame you," I say. "What do you mean that Cliff was going to announce who he would sell it to? You mean he was keeping that a secret?"

"It wasn't so much a secret," Melanie said, "as that he didn't actually know. He was having a hard time deciding between the two bidders: Joe and Ralph. They both wanted to buy the restaurant from him."

"Ralph, his assistant?" I ask.

"Yes," Melanie says. A dark shadow crosses her face. "Ralph." Her voice drips with disdain.

She stirs her coffee, but still doesn't take a sip. I'm almost done with mine. My mind is working double-time.

I speak aloud as I try to work through the possibilities. "If Ralph *and* Joe were both in the running to own the restaurant, was Ralph happy when Joe was found dead?" I muse. "Could he have killed Joe, so that he could own the restaurant?"

"Wait a minute," Melanie says. "You think Joe was *killed*?"

"It's definitely a possibility," I say. "That's what I learned in PI school. Means plus a strong enough motive equals murder. It was one of the formulas we had to commit to memory."

Melanie's quiet, so I keep talking. "That's a pretty major motivator, don't you think? Ralph has been in your husband's shadow for years. Maybe he felt that if he owned the restaurant, he would finally be in the spotlight. What is he like?" I ask.

"Ug," she says, making a disgusted sound.

"You're… you're not a fan?" I say, interpreting her grunted communication.

"Ralph and I don't get along," Melanie says. "*Why* my husband insists on working with such a sleazy man is beyond me. Cliff goes on about Ralph's work ethics and attention to details," Melanie scoffs. "But does that matter, if a person is rotten to the core? If I was the mayor, I'd rather deal with a few administrative slip ups now and then, than having a weasel as my right hand."

Interesting.

Before I can ask more about Ralph, Melanie says, "Enough about him, though. I don't like to speak poorly of people. It's not attractive, you know."

She glances at her watch. "Speaking of attractive, I have a hair appointment at eleven thirty. I'm going to be late. If I don't get my roots done, I feel like a slob."

Taking the hint, I stand. With a whirlwind of activity, Melanie cleans up the coffee mugs, creamer, sugar, and napkins, and gives the countertops a quick wipe down. She really is a housekeeper extraordinaire.

While she's occupied with her frenzy, I take a peek at a neat pile of notebooks and magazines, positioned in a little metal organizational bin at one end of the countertop.

The book on the top of the pile is leather bound, and looks like a planner. I can see little tabs announcing the days of the months, sticking out from one side.

I want to badly flip it open and take a glance at August. I'm not sure if the book is Melanie's or Cliff's, but either way the information inside might be helpful.

Melanie snaps off the coffee pot and then begins ushering me to towards the door. I intentionally leave my messenger bag on the floor by the stool I've been sitting on.

"Thank you for your time," I say, as we reach the front gate.

"Well," she sighs dramatically. "It couldn't be avoided. I hope that I answered all of your questions."

I can read between the lines: She's hoping that she won't have to endure another interview with me.

"I think so," I say. "If anything else comes up, I'll be sure to reach out to you."

She frowns and opens her mouth, but I set off towards my bike before she can protest. "Bye, Melanie!" I call out.

I linger around on my bike, watching her round the corner. Then, I make my way back through her gate. Surely Melanie wouldn't mind if I let myself in, just to grab my forgotten bag?

I feel clever! I reach the kitchen. Before collecting my bag, I walk over to the leather bound planner and take a quick peek inside. I locate the September tab, and flip open to a calendar.

With one look at the pink, cursive writing, I know that I've got Melanie's planner in my hands. A quick look at the first of September confirms this: *'Hair appointment -- touch up roots -- 11:30'* it says.

I'm almost one hundred percent certain that Cliff Haywater doesn't write in pink, cursive lettering about dying his roots.

I flip to the August calendar and my eyes track over to the little box that represents the fourteenth.

There's only one item listed. *'Pick up from Bess -- 2:30,'* it says. There's a little heart next to the note, but no further details.

Since I'm starting to get freaked out about being in the Haywater's home uninvited, I close the planner, scoop up my bag, and hustle to the door.

I make my way back to my office, and spend the afternoon trying to organize my thoughts on the case. I crowd my notebook page with details that I've learned, but it only serves to make me more confused. How does a one-way ticket to Hawaii connect to a rotten, weasel-like personal assistant?

Furthermore, why wouldn't Melanie mention that she had to visit Bess' Antique Haven?

She was hiding something, when she gave me her timeline of the day. It seemed that my peek into her planner explained what she was hiding: a visit to Bess, at the Antique Haven. Why would she lie?

And if she lied about a visit to Bess, what *else* was she lying about?

Chapter Four

That evening, at five o'clock on the nose, I ride up to my friend Annie's cafe. Unlike Melanie, I am not perfectly organized, nor averse to being late. In fact, I'm *usually* late for things.

My Wednesday evening knitting circle is an exception.

I'm *never* late for knitting circle.

I pull open the door to the Death Cafe.

Yep, that's the name of Annie's business, and she has no plans, as far as I know, to change it. Annie re-named it in July, after what my friend Marley termed an 'end-of-life crisis'. Instead of the red-sports car purchasing symptoms of a mid-life crisis, her end-of-life crisis consisted of a campaign to normalize the word Death.

I'm pretty sure she didn't consult any marketing experts, when she decided on the new name. However, since the residents of Hillcrest are highly addicted to her coffee and sugary, freshly baked treats, business has been doing just fine -- despite the perhaps off-putting name.

Though, I've become kind of attached to the name, over the past few months. And strangely enough, it *has* removed some of my own fear around the word Death.

Now, when I think of the word Death, I think of iced americanos, confectioners-sugar dusted lemon squares, and conversations with friends.

Her campaign, at least for me, has been a success.

I enter the cafe and see that the other members of the knitting circle are already seated around a table in the middle of the cafe. I'm not the only one who arrives on time -- we all prioritize this gathering.

Annie always closes down at four, so our knitting group has the place to ourselves. The inside of the cafe looks nothing like you might expect, given the morbid name. Annie has painted the walls bright, sunshine yellow and the many tables scattered around the room are draped in white table cloths. Paintings of flowers, along with copious bouquets scattered around the room, complete the cheerful vibe.

Marley waves as I enter.

"Hey, girl!" she says.

She's wearing a tank top and loose overalls. Her glossy black hair lies in a braided rope over one shoulder. I've always admired Marley's pretty hair -- ever since we were kindergarteners together.

In fact, I've always admired everything about Marley; from her shiny hair to her perfectly proportioned figure, to her carefree lifestyle. Marley lives in a red and white VW van, parked on the edge of town.

"The dragonfly wings finally came in!" she says, flashing a bright smile.

I have my knitting tote bag slung over my shoulder, along with my messenger bag, so I take a moment to unburden myself. Then I flop down into a chair and reach for a pitcher of lemonade that Annie has placed in the middle of the table.

Marley continues. "Cora picked them up at the post office this morning. Show her, Cora!"

Cora is beaming as she holds up a little, tiny plastic bag, and shakes it a little bit. "The packaging even says, 'no dragonflies were harmed in the collection of these wings.' Isn't that great?" she says happily.

"So, they were already dead when the wings were plucked off?" Annie asks. She's already knitting, and her fingers fly as though the act is as natural as breathing. I hope to be as skilled a knitter as Annie is, one day.

I pull out my Icelandic sweater pattern, along with the blue, yellow and grey wool and my needles. Then, I pull out my copy of ASBW. Marley, Cora and Annie already have their copies out in front of them.

"Is that going to work?" I ask. "Does the book specify if the dragonflies have to be dead or alive when the wings are removed?"

"I hope not," Cora says, making a face. "I don't want to do a spell if it includes torturing innocent dragonflies."

"Neither do I," Marley says.

I flip to the first page of cycle one and scan the words. "Nope," I say. "It just says 'dragonfly wings'."

"Thank goodness," says Annie.

Cora sets down the bag gently. "I'm going to postulate that these wings were collected off dragonflies that died naturally after living very full, happy lives," she says primly.

Whereas Marley and I sometimes act like kids trapped in adult bodies, Cora is a true, mature grown up. She has a house, drives a compact SUV, and when she drops an ice cube, she doesn't kick it under the fridge. I bet she even flosses every night. Though she's only ten years older than me, she's a mother figure in my life.

"What else was it that we were waiting on?" Annie asks. She keeps knitting as she looks over the photocopied page in front of her. Her reading glasses are propped low on her nose, and her halo of short, curly, white hair bobs up and down slightly as she knits.

"Okay… let's see. Cycle One. The Power Spell," she says, reading aloud. "The first cycle of magic that you will embark on in your initiation into witchcraft consists of learning about the power within you. In order to do so, follow the steps to this power potion precisely."

She pauses to take a breath. Marley, Cora and I are all listening intently, though we've heard and read the directions many times over the past few months.

Annie continues reading. "Remember -- these objects are only symbols for what is occurring within you. As you combine them, reflect upon what they represent, as outlined below. Once you have gathered and combined these powerful symbols from the richness of Mother Earth, you will then wear them in a satchel around your neck for - - "

"What is a satchel, exactly?" Marley asks.

"We've gone over this before," Cora says with a sigh. "It's like a little purse."

"Should we order some online now?" I ask. "We should have done it when we ordered the dragonfly wings? I bet Etsy has satchels, too."

"That will only give us another delay," Annie says, shaking her head. "We've already spent long enough gathering up the other supplies. I vote that we sew the satchels ourselves. It won't take more than a half an hour."

"Agreed," Cora says. "We've really gotten behind on this cycle. Who would have ever guessed it would take us over two months!"

"Good point," I say. "I'm up for sewing."

"Me too," Marley says.

"That settles it," Annie says. "It is unanimous: We shall sew our own satchels."

As a coven, we're a very democratic bunch.

Annie speaks up again. "Now, we just have to decide if we want to do that little project tonight, or next week. If we want to make them tonight, I do have some old curtains that I pulled down with the remodel. Perhaps not the most aesthetically pleasing print, but they would certainly do the job." She looks around at us. "I also have needles and thread. All in favor of tonight?" she asks.

Again, it's unanimous. We all want to get this Power Spell show on the road. Annie slips away to gather the supplies. While she's gone, Cora points to the sweater pattern in front of me, along with the three still-wrapped skeins of yarn.

"Penny," she says. "I thought you were planning on starting your sweater this week. What happened?"

I look at the unstarted project. "I couldn't," I say. "I just kept working on that scarf I have going."

"How long is that thing now?" Marley says, laughing.

"Too long," I say, rolling my eyes. "But it's easy. I know the pattern by heart."

"Because you've made a *million* scarves," says Marley.

"Not a million!" I protest.

"Penny, you're ready to try something new. You're getting really good!" Cora says.

"Thanks," I say, somewhat unenthusiastically. "This sweater is going to be a lot harder than the scarves. It's going to take my full focus, and I've been a bit distracted these few days."

"Because Max is back in town?" guesses Cora.

"Did you finally spend the night at Chris's?" guesses Marley.

"No!" I say. "This isn't about Chris. Or Max. I'm distracted about *work*. I have a new case." Then, because I'm curious, I ask Cora. "How did you know Max was back in town?"

"Oh, he came into the law offices," she says casually.

Cora is the administrative assistant to the new lawyer in town, a woman by the name of Hiroku Itsu. "He wanted to meet with Hiroku to go over the details of a lease. It was for an apartment over in your area, Penny. Blackbear Apartments. Unit B, I think it was."

I gulp. "That isn't in my 'area', Cora. That's *right* below me."

Cora laughs. "Don't worry. I don't think he ended up signing it. Someone else signed the lease first. What's your new case?"

"It has to do with the Haywaters," I say. "Just between us, I don't think their marriage is going that great."

"Well, that's not new news," Cora says. "Anyone can see they're not happy. Haven't been for years, in my opinion. And, since we're keeping things between us here," she lowers her voice, though no one else is in the cafe, "I think Melanie was getting divorce papers from Hiroku. They've had several meetings, and I *happened* to overhear the word 'divorce' a few times."

"Really?" I ask. This is useful information! Being friends with a gabby law-office secretary has once again paid off. "Any idea when the divorce was supposed to go through?"

"I think it is imminent," Cora says. "Usually, when people meet with a lawyer about that sort of thing, they mean business. I'm actually surprised we haven't heard anything about it yet. News of a break-up spreads so fast in this town. The meetings were happening weeks ago, so I thought we'd be hearing whispers by now."

"She's still living at the house," I say. "And Cliff doesn't seem to have any idea about a divorce. At least, he didn't mention it to me, and he seemed to think that the marriage would benefit from a shared vacation."

Cora shakes her head. She's busily working on a pair of legwarmers. "That would be a *disaster*," she says, as her needles click rhythmically.

"Sounds like he's clueless," Marley says, while pouring herself a glass of lemonade.

"Poor guy," Cora adds. "Sometimes that's how it goes, though. I've seen it happen in the law office before. One partner wants out, but they want to get all their ducks in a row before bringing it up with the other partner. Seems cold, but it happens."

Annie returns to the table, carrying a folded curtain and a little wicker box of knitting supplies "What seems cold?" she asks.

"When a husband or wife talks to a lawyer about divorce, before actually talking to their spouse," I say.

"Cold, indeed" Annie says with a nod. She sets the supplies down on the table, in the spot that Cora cleared for her.

Cora reaches for the folded curtain fabric and spreads it out.

"None of us have husbands," Annie says. "Why are we talking about divorce?"

"I'm working on a new case," I say. "It involved the Haywaters. Cora was just saying that she thinks they're headed for a divorce. Melanie's been visiting the law office."

"Just between us," Cora says.

"I see," Annie says. "Such a shame." She removes shears, a pin cushion, and two spools of thread from the wicker box. "Poor Melanie. She comes into the cafe often, and she hasn't seemed well these days."

I speak up. "I think she's still upset over the whole Joe Gallant thing. You know, how he was found in the deep freezer?"

"What a terrible accident," Cora says. Annie hands her the scissors, and she begins carefully cutting out four squares of fabric

"I'm not so sure it was an accident," I say.

This gets everyone's rapt attention. Cora stops cutting. Marley puts down her glass of lemonade, and Annie sets down the spool of thread in her hands.

"What do you mean?" asks Marley.

"I *mean*, I think Joe Gallant was murdered," I say. "I think someone either forced him into that freezer or waited until he was inside, and then held the door shut while he died."

"You have a dark mind," Cora says. She resumes cutting

"I have a *realistic* mind," I say. "Cliff said that he never had any issues with the freezer. I don't think it would just malfunction like that, on the *last* day that Cliff owned the restaurant, and the day right before Melanie was supposed to take off for Hawaii."

"Melanie was going to Hawaii?" Annie asks.

I nod. "She bought a ticket. For the fifteenth. Joe died on the fourteenth. Isn't the timing strange?"

"I've always wanted to go to Hawaii," Annie says. "My husband and I were going to go, for our fiftieth anniversary."

We all fall silent.

Annie's husband passed away years ago, before the anniversary date ever occurred.

After a respectful silence, Marley chimes in. "I've always wanted to see Hawaii too. The weather is supposed to be perfect."

"I love the ocean," Cora says, dreamily.

"It is odd that the freezer went on the fritz while someone was in it, after years of working perfectly," Annie says. "You really think someone tinkered with it?"

"I really do," I respond.

"Who would do such a malicious thing?" Marley asks, while Cora passes out squares of fabric.

I accept mine. It's pale blue, with little white and pink flowers printed on it. The print is faded, from years of soaking up sunshine. It's a drab fabric, all in all, but it will do the job. Annie passes me a threaded needle.

As I fold the little square of fabric in half, I recite the list I've been pondering all day. "I have four suspects," I say. "All these people went into the restaurant on the day that Joe was found dead. Ralph, Glenn, Cliff and Melanie."

"Look at you, with your little list of suspects! You sound like a real detective," Marley says.

"I *am* a real detective!" I say.

Annie is already sewing her satchel, and I peek over to make sure I'm on the right track.

Nope.

She's folded one edge in just a few millimeters and is pinning it in place.

"For the drawstring to go through," she says, as she spots me peeking.

"Oh! Right, I say, as I unfold my square and then copy her.

Soon we're all sewing. The conversation centers around my case for quite some time. I let the ladies know all that I was able to glean from Melanie. Once I've recounted the interview in entirety, my friends add in their two cents.

"She's definitely lying," Marley says.

Annie nods sagely. "Yes, it's odd that she didn't want to tell you about going to Bess's Antique Haven."

"Maybe she just forgot?" guesses Cora.

Annie shakes her head. "Melanie has an excellent memory. Once I served her a regular latte instead of a decaf, and she brings it up *every time* she comes in. That happened five years back. That woman's mind is like a steel trap."

"I think she is hiding it on purpose," I agree. "She acted super sketchy when she talked about the span of time between leaving the retirement party in the park, and then going to The Place. She wouldn't meet my eye. I wish I knew why she would lie to me about that."

"Maybe the Power Spell will help," suggests Cora. She holds up her perfectly sewn satchel. "Let's fill these babies up!"

Chapter Five

Cora waves her satchel in the air, showing it off to the group. I'm done also, so I hold it up as well. Mine looks a little bit crooked, but it will have to do.

"It *would* be nice to feel more powerful," I say. "This case is a little bit above and beyond what I'm used to."

"You did an excellent job with the candy bar theft," Annie says, reaching over and patting my forearm. "Don't discredit yourself."

"Thanks," I say.

Annie sets aside her own satchel, which is also now done. She pulls forward her photocopied ASBW pages. "I think it would be helpful for all of us to feel more powerful," she says. "We *are* a coven of witches, in charge of protecting a portal into our little town, after all. If we don't figure out how to harness this power, I have the distinct feeling that things could get wild here, very quickly."

I know what she means.

I have the same feeling.

When Claudine Terra died, the mountain pass behind her house mysteriously opened up to through traffic. It turned out that Claudine had been protecting Hillcrest from visitors of other magical realms. Now that she's gone, it's up to Annie, Cora, Marley and I to monitor the pass and protect the town. I have to admit, we've been doing a very spotty job of it, so far.

"Thank goodness the pass has been so quiet," I say. "There haven't really been any magical visitors, have there?"

"Except for Max," Cora says.

"Well, yeah. But he's safe."

"Is he?" Cora asks. She lifts a brow and looks pointedly at me. "I feel like, at least for *one* of us, he's a very dangerous visitor."

"Dangerously tempting," Marley adds, wiggling her eyebrows my way.

Annie clears her throat. "Ladies… I do like talking about handsome men, but if we don't progress with our witch abilities, we may encounter beings that are more than just dangerously good looking," Annie looks very grandmotherly as she peers around the table at us through her reading glasses. "I don't like it that the portal is open, and we're still so inept. It makes me feel like a sitting duck."

"Me too," says Marley. "I've been having a strange feeling lately. Like trouble is brewing."

"Okay," I say. "Then it's really time for us to put this spell together. Maybe once we've done the Power Spell, I'll be able to figure out who killed Joe, *and* we'll be better prepared as guardians of the portal."

"Well put," Annie says. "Now, what are we going to do about this secret key ingredient nonsense?"

"Ug," Marley says.

"*That*," Cora says.

"I have no idea," I add in.

There is one part of the Power Spell that has been hanging us up for weeks. Months, in fact. We can't seem to get past it. It's slowing us down more than even the dragonfly wings or the satchels. Actually, we would have figured *those* roadblocks out much sooner, if we'd been more motivated. But our motivation was zapped by an item at the bottom of the list of ingredients, that has us stumped.

It has been stealing the wind from our sails, since we started the cycle.

For the hundredth time, I read over the instructions for the Power Spell.

*Cycle One.
The Power Spell*

The first cycle of magic that you will embark on in your initiation into witchcraft consists of learning about the power within you. In order to do so, follow the steps to this power potion precisely.

Remember -- these objects are only symbols for what is occurring within you. As you combine them, reflect upon what they represent (as outlined below). Once you have gathered and combined these powerful symbols from the richness of Mother Earth, you will then wear them in a satchel around your neck until the spell is complete.

You will know when the Power Spell is completed.

A feeling of power as you have never experienced before will be born inside of you. It is impossible to express this in words. You will know it when you feel it.

Once again, remember to follow these instructions with precision. This is one of the cornerstones of witchcraft. Always remember the three p's: Patience, Precision, and Playfulness.

Ingredients:

½ tsp. Earth (dry, fine dirt works best. From your location is preferable). This represents your connection to Mother Earth -- a great source of strength.

3 Dragonfly wings -- three sets. This symbol represents your ability to change, adapt, transform, and realize your true Self.

¼ tsp Ash -- This represents your inner fire.

The fur of a feline - three hairs, at least three millimeters in length, to represent the fearlessness of a lion.

Secret Key Ingredient -- this depends on the witch. Every witch has his or her own specific, individualized Secret Key Ingredient. No one can tell you what yours is. You must intuitively figure it out. Once you have figured it out, write it down in your Book of Shadows and meditate upon it for twenty-one days after the spell begins to function. You will feel your power increase as you marinate in your special, secret key ingredient.

Directions.
Grind dragonfly wings with a mortar and pestle for three minutes, until they form a fine powder. Mix in the sand. Next, add in your ash*. Add in the feline fur. Pour the contents into your satchel.

It is important that you wear this around your neck -- even while you sleep -- until the magic begins to work. Enjoy the results!

*Note: This ash should be prepared ahead of time, by burning a piece of paper on which you have listed your biggest fear.

I look up. The other women are also staring at their copies of ASBW, puzzling over the words.

"Well, at least we already made our ashes," Marley says. "That step's done. I'm worried about this whole Secret Key Ingredient thing. What if I can't figure mine out, and I'm stuck wearing this ugly pouch full of cat hairs and dirt for the rest of my life?"

"I'm not going to do that," Cora says. "This is grossing me out as it is. Dead bugs, cat hair... I don't even want this to be in my *house*, let alone around my neck. If this doesn't work in a few days, I'm going to throw the whole thing out."

"It *is* going to work," I say, resolutely. "Everything else in the book has been true for us, right? We've all experienced things that we didn't know were possible, before."

"True," Cora says.

I continue. "We can't give up now, you guys. We're just starting out with all of this. We're on cycle one, of thirteen! If we start losing faith now, there's no way we're going to finish with all the cycles. We'll be stuck in this kind of in-between phase -- caught in between being a human and being a witch."

"It's like being in puberty," Marley says grumpily.

"I hated puberty," Cora says.

I continue. "If we don't trust the book, we're never going to become the witches that we're destined to be. This is the beginning stages, of *course* it feels weird. But if we keep doing what it says, we'll get to experience it working. It's like the book says, words can't explain what it will be like to step into our new lives. We're going to have to *feel* it. And that means following the steps and trusting that it will work."

All of us nod.

Cora rummages in her bag, and pulls out a mortar and pestle. "Who wants to go first?" she asks.

I remember back when my mom was alive, and we used to make ice-cream by hand. We used to take turns turning the handle to spin the cream and sugar within the metal contraption. For the next half hour, I'm reminded of those evenings with my mother.

Annie, Cora, Marley and I take turns grinding up our dragonfly wings, and then mixing in dirt, ash, and cat hair. By the time I put my own ingredients into my pouch, I'm feeling very nostalgic. I'm grateful for the women around me. If it wasn't for them, the memory of my mother would make me feel lonely. Now, I feel like I'm surrounded by family.

When I place my new necklace around my neck, I have a feeling of excitement.

The last part of the spell involves holding hands around the table. It is dark now, and Annie has lit a candle in the middle of the table. The flame flickers across my friends faces. I'm filled with a pleasant feeling of warmth, sisterhood, and gratitude.

We recite the incantation that's printed below the spell directions, in unison:

"Witch sisters from high,
Witch sisters from low
Help these new witches
Declare it is so

Witch brothers with eyes
Witch brothers with heart
Help these new witches
Thrive from the start

The power within
Will soon be evoked
The power among us
So soon will be yoked

As each of us harness
our magical powers

The magical seconds
become magical hours

The magical hours
turn to magical days
And each string together
to form magic that stays"

When our recitation ends, I feel that I can't let go of Marley's hand, nor Cora's. There is a charge running through us. It zips in from one side of my body, flows through me, and out towards Cora. I have goosebumps all over my arms

Then, the candle flickers out, all of a sudden. At the same time, the energy flowing through my hands stops, and I feel unstuck. I let go of my friends' hands, just as they let go of mine.

"Must have been a draft," Annie says. There's a stream of wispy smoke curling up from the candle.

"Yeah, must have," Marley says. She sounds as shaken as I feel. The lights behind the counter are on, so it isn't *entirely* dark in the cafe, but still, the candle going out just as we finished reading aloud felt spooky.

I wonder if anyone else noticed the feeling of energy in their hands, but I'm too spooked to ask. I have the distinct desire to talk about something that *doesn't* involve witchcraft. I've traveled about as far out of my comfort zone as I'm prepared to go, tonight.

"Well, we didn't get much knitting done, did we?" I say.

"Nope," Cora says with a nervous laugh. I can tell she's spooked too.

Annie begins tidying up, and we all start to help.

As Annie consolidates baked goods onto one plate, she says. "Well, Penny if you want any help getting your sweater started before our next meeting, just stop by the cafe."

"Thanks," I say. "I'm not sure how far I'll get with it. I'm going to be pretty busy with the Haywater case."

"Let me know if you need a detective sidekick, Penny," says Marley. "I'm free tomorrow."

"And I can see what I can dig up about Melanie's divorce papers," Cora says.

"I'll keep my ear to the ground, at the cafe," Annie adds.

"Thanks guys," I say. "I really appreciate the help." I give my necklace a pat. "Maybe this spell will kick in soon and give us a boost, too."

After saying goodnight, we part ways.

By the time I ride my bike home and reach my apartment, it's seven thirty. Chris is working late, so it's just Turkey and I for the evening.

To make up for keeping Turkey up last night with loud music, I give him extra Finicky Feline Feast on top of his dry food. Then, we both go to bed early. I read for a half an hour, and by eight thirty, my heavy eyelids are drifting closed.

Hopefully I'll get a good night of sleep. I want to be on top of my game tomorrow. I'm not sure if I'll track down Ralph or pay a visit to Bess at the Antique Haven. Either way, I want to be feeling sharp.

Who knows? I could crack this case tomorrow.

I know it's probably wishful thinking, but what's wrong with making a wish now and then?

If I can cast spells, I sure as heck can make wishes. Wishes are easy: there's no assembly required.

With one hand on my necklace and a last look at the stars outside of my window, I fall into a deep sleep.

Chapter Six

The next day, I wake up bright and early, from a vivid dream about soaring above the clouds. As my eyes adjust to the bright morning light, I can still see the puffy white clouds in my mind's eye.

I haven't had a dream *that* vivid in a long time.

After pulling myself from bed and shuffling to the living room, I put the three hundred dollars that Cliff gave me into an envelope and promise myself that I'll deliver it to Sherry O'Neil before the day's end. I also make a grocery list and vow to get grocery shopping checked off my to-do list as well. I'm tired of living on dry choco-puffs and black coffee.

I haven't done laundry in over a week. Since I'm feeling well-rested and productive, I load up the washing machine.

It turns out that I get a little bit overzealous, and throw pretty much my whole wardrobe in. This makes it hard to get dressed, but after digging into the very back of my closet, I manage to find an outfit that will work. It's comprised of clothes I used to wear before I lost a bunch of weight with weekly Zumba sweat-sessions, so everything's a bit baggy, but it will have to do. One good thing is that the black cable-knit dress is nice and cozy, which will feel good given the crisp fall weather.

I'm still wearing my little pouch of spell ingredients, and I tuck it safely beneath the cozy dress. I finish the outfit with my leopard-print framed fake glasses, so that I'll feel smart throughout the day.

By nine, I'm heading out the door.

I haven't yet decided which lead to pursue -- talk to Ralph or check out Bess's Antique Haven -- but I figure I'll get started with a visit to my office. There I can collect my thoughts, and hopefully I'll run into Sherry as well. It would be nice to check off the 'pay rent' box on my to-do list.

I haven't quite reached my office when I start to sense that someone is watching me. I roll to a stop and put both feet on the ground before carefully look over my shoulder.

This is because I've gotten into accidents before, when I look over my shoulder while riding. I'm not the most coordinated person in the world, and when I try to turn around while riding, I tend to turn the whole front tire with me -- which isn't good. I've fallen more than once.

When I finally manage to look behind me, I see Chris. He's in his police car, creeping along silently behind me. As I turn, he leans out the window. "Hey there cutie," he says.

"Chris! You scared me."

"I didn't mean to." He parks the car and gets out. He's dressed in his police uniform. He looks so handsome in the navy blue cargo pants, button up shirt, and official badge. As he approaches my bike, he says, "I saw a pretty girl on a bike, and I couldn't help but follow her."

"Do you do that often?" I ask, feigning distaste. "That's creepy."

He grins. "Nah," he says. "I only follow *you*. Heading into your supply closet?"

"Office," I say, glaring. "Yes. Are you working a day shift? Want to hang out tonight?" I'm thinking about another make-out session on the couch. Nothing helps a stressed PI unwind like a good make-out session. Nope, I didn't learn that in Speedy's Online Private Investigator Licensure Program. I discovered it all on my own.

Chris seems to be thinking about our habitual late-night activities as well, because he grins. "Sounds good to me," he says knowingly. "I'll bring over some beer."

"And pizza," I say. "Don't forget the pizza." I need a back-up plan, in case I don't make it to the grocery store.

"On it," Chris says. Then, his joking demeanor fades. He becomes more serious. "Hey," he says. "I was thinking about what you said... about me not having respect for your PI business?"

I can't quite recall saying that, but I'll take his word for it. Chris is always acting like I'm clueless when it comes to fighting crime. Maybe it's because I once shot his arm, back when I was a student in his class at police academy.

"Yeah?" I say, prompting him to say more. "What were you thinking?" I ask.

His blue-grey eyes are gazing at me, full of sincerity. "I was thinking that wasn't very nice of me. I'm your *boyfriend*. I should be supportive of you. So... I got you something."

"You did?" For some reason, I still get heart-palpitations when Chris talks about being my boyfriend. I think it's because for so many years, when I was younger, I fantasized about Christopher Wagner. Now, it's like that young teen who still lives inside of me can hardly believe we're actually dating. She's in there somewhere, pinching herself to make sure she's not dreaming.

Chris walks to his cop car. I get off my bike, and stand, waiting for him to return. My heart continues to flutter.

What in the world did he get me?

The fluttering sensation in my chest increases when I see a little box in his hands.

It looks like a jewelry box.

Did he get me a necklace or something?

Or worse... a ring?

Or -- I feel like I might pass out now -- an *engagement* ring?

Does he want to show his support by *proposing* to me? My mouth turns all cottony and dry, and I feel like I can't swallow. No. It can't be an engagement ring. That would be *insane*. It can't be.

Could it?

What if he asks me to marry him?

What would I say?

I'm having trouble breathing. I stand stock still as he returns to me, with the little box in his hand.

Without fanfare, he holds it out to me.

He wouldn't do that if it was an engagement ring. He'd be down on one knee. Or does that only happen in the movies? Maybe this is a Chris-casual proposal. *'Yeah, I'll bring over pizza and beer. Oh yeah, and hey, by the way, want to be my wife?'*

Oh, great. Now I feel nauseous.

"Penny?" Chris says. "Are you going to open it?"

I'm just standing here, holding the box in one hand, and my bike in the other. Carefully, I lean my bike against my hip and place both hands on the box. I take a deep breath. Please, don't let this be a ring, I pray. Then, I pull off the lid.

Thank Goddess. It's not a ring!

It's a little silver key.

I lift it up, and morning sunlight sparkles off it. "What is this?" I ask.

For a brief instant, I wonder if he's going to say something cheesy, like, *'It's the key to my heart,'* or something. But that's not like Chris. He's not really the romantic type.

His grin broadens. "It goes with these," he says, reaching into his cargo pocket and pulling out a pair of handcuffs.

"Woah!" Now it's my turn to grin. I was nervous about receiving jewelry from Chris, especially the kind that would fit on my left ring finger. But handcuffs? This I can handle.

I reach for the cuffs.

"I thought it would be good for you to have a pair," Chris says. "It's wrong of me to belittle what you do. Hopefully, you'll never have to use these, but if you're ever doing surveillance for a job and witness a felony, you might need to do a citizen arrest. You should have the right tools."

"Thank you," I say, in utter awe. Now I have a gun *and* handcuffs. How official do I feel? Very! One of these days I'll get around to ordering some business cards. I have been saying that for the past five years, but I'm feeling very confident that it's going to happen soon.

"Do you know how to use them?" Chris asks.

I'm examining the cuffs. "It can't be that hard," I say. "Right? I just slap them on the person and like, lock them up somehow?"

Chris shakes his head. "It would be nice if it was that easy. But if you were to use cuffs, it's because you're in a really dangerous situation. You're detaining the person while you wait for the proper authorities to arrive and you can bet they're not going to just sit there nice and pretty while you restrain them. You need to know the body mechanics of getting someone into the right position to get the cuffs on."

"How do I do that?" I ask.

"I could show you," Chris says. "What are you doing now? We could take a ride over to the park. It's been a slow morning."

I laugh, thinking of being in Town Park with Chris, as he shows me various tackling techniques. "Great -- you and I out in public, wrestling each other to the ground and then using handcuffs. What will the dog-walkers have to say about that? I can just imagine the stories that would start churning through the rumor mill," I say.

He catches on, and chuckles. "Right," he says. "Better not do that. What about somewhere more out of the way?"

I think this over. I have a lot to do today, but how could I say no to a free lesson on how to place handcuffs, from the Hillcrest Police Department Captain? It's an added bonus that he's extremely handsome and happens to be my boyfriend. Maybe I don't have to wait until tonight to enjoy a little physical intimacy.

"How about up Mill Creek Road?" I suggest. "There's a clearing up there, and it's usually deserted."

"Mill Creek it is," he says. "I'll drive."

I lock my bike to a nearby signpost. Then I toss my messenger bag into the back seat of Chris's patrol car, before climbing into the passenger seat.

Back when I was in the Police Academy, I used to imagine what it would be like, to be Chris's police officer partner. I imagined the two of us, cruising the streets of Hillcrest.

Since Police Academy was such a disaster for me, that never happened. However, here I am, sitting in his cruiser as his detective girlfriend. Not bad!

I'm feeling pretty pleased with myself as we drive up the long, winding dirt road. When Chris parks, I remove my fake glasses and stash them on the dashboard. I don't want them to fall off and get lost when I'm tackling Chris. Then I spring out of the car, and jog into the open meadow. The crisp blue autumn sky is filled with little white puffy clouds. Birds sing from the tall pagosa pines that line the clearing.

The teenager inside of me is still pinching herself as I watch Chris cross the meadow towards me.

"Alright," he says. "Lesson number one. If you're in a situation where you need to use cuffs, it's because a person has committed a felony -- we're talking armed robbery, assault, or worse -- and they're clearly dangerous. Handcuffs are just a temporary restraining device. Even when they're on a person, you should consider that person a threat."

"Because they can still kick, right?" I ask.

"Or spit, or head-butt you, or a number of other things," Chris says. "Believe me. I've seen it all."

"Lovely," I say.

"You want to be prepared," Chris says. "You have to be really wary, while you're putting the cuffs on, while they're on, and when you're taking them off."

"Got it," I say.

"Okay. We're going to pretend that I'm your target. Say you're in a situation where you need to detain someone, while you wait for the police to arrive. I'll be your suspect. But first, let's run through how you lock and unlock them."

He positions himself close to me. "You want to start with them in the 'loaded' position," he says. "With that little lever engaged." He leans down and points to a small lever on the cuffs. "Then, they're ready to be used."

He places his large hand over mine and helps me flip a release switch.

It's easy. It can be done one handed. I have the little key in my other hand.

"Should I try unlocking it?" I ask.

"Yeah," Chris answers. "Stick the key there." He points to a little keyhole. "And give it a twist."

I do, and the cuffs spring open once again. Chris pulls out the key and hands it back to me. "Pretty simple, right?" he says.

I nod, dreamily. Even though it's hard to focus with him standing so close to me, I totally understand the simple steps he's just shown me.

I can't help but tilt my chin up and give him a quick kiss. "This is fun," I say softly, as he continues to stand close.

He shifts his body and begins to hold me in earnest.

For an instant, we forget all about the cuffs.

"Everything is fun with you, Penny," he says.

I laugh, giddily. When he holds me like this, I feel like I'm melting. To show him how good it feels to be held, I wrap my arms around his neck. I have the cuffs in one hand, and the key in the other. I press my body against Chris's and we kiss like that for minutes on end.

By the time we pull ourselves apart, we're both smiling dreamily.

"What's next, Captain Wagner?" I ask.

"Okay," Chris says. "We'll pretend that I'm your target, and I'm combative. I won't be, really, but treat me as though I might throw a punch or a kick at any moment. Just get me to the point where you've got my arms behind my back. We'll run through this a couple of times."

"Should I put the cuffs on you, once I've got you in position?" I ask.

"We'll get to that after," Chris says. "For right now, let's practice without them."

I set down the handcuffs and key on the grass, and then for the next hour Chris and I run around the meadow, taking turns play fighting each other. I get good at getting his hands behind his back, though I'm sure in part it's because he's letting me.

Our practice session dissolves into the both of us lying on our backs. Chris has his arms around me, and my head is on his chest. We're breathless, partly from kissing and partly from our play fighting.

As I look up at the clouds, I ask, "Are you sure you have time for this? Should we head back to town soon?"

"I guess we *should*," Chris says, rolling over me, so that he's pinning me down. "But then how would you learn to take down a criminal? Look, I just got you again."

"Not fair!" I protest. "I wasn't ready."

He leans down and kisses me. It's a deep, passionate kiss. I wasn't ready for *that*, either.

When the kiss ends, I roll on top of him. "Ha!" I say. "Got you!"

He laughs, and starts tickling me.

"You are such a cheater!" I cry, before managing to get to my feet.

When we're both standing, I spot the cuffs on the ground, a foot away. "Can I try putting them on you, just once before we head back?" I ask.

"Sure," says Chris. He flips back into cop mode. "When you're carrying them, you're going to want to make sure they're in the loaded position, like I showed you. You don't want to get your target into position and then have to mess around with setting up your cuffs. You want them to be all set to snap on."

"Okay," I say, picking up the set.

"Keep your key somewhere safe," Chris says. "I keep mine on my key ring."

"I don't have a car," I say.

"But you have a key to your apartment, right?" says Chris. "You must have a key ring."

"Nope," I say. "I don't usually lock up my place during the day."

"You don't?" Chris looks appalled. "You should. Okay, maybe get some kind of a keyring, and put something big and obvious on it, like a tennis ball. Something you won't lose. You *don't* want to lose that key." He points to it. "I got these cuffs second hand from a guy in Melrose. He lost the spare. That's the only key."

"Got it," I say. "I'll get a keyring and an impossible to lose keychain."

"For now just stick the key in your pocket," Chris says. "And keep the cuffs in one hand. You really want to be able to put them on fast. I'll go over here, and you pretend that you're apprehending me. Okay?"

"Okay," I say.

Chris turns and starts walking away. My dress doesn't have any pockets, so I stick the key in my bra. Then, I run after Chris.

He dodges me, and for a minute or two we circle each other. Then, I manage to do a few of the moves he's taught me, and I get him to the ground. Soon I have his hands behind his back, and I snap the cuffs onto him.

He sits up. "Nice work!" he says. "I feel like I'm at the training center with the other cops. You're athletic, Penny."

"I was always the last picked in gym class," I say.

"That's just because of your confidence," he says. "You're not the most self-confident person. But you're coordinated. You're better than half of the other officers on the Hillcrest PD."

Since there are four officers, that means I'm better than two of them. It's not much, but I'll take it!

"Really?" I ask. "You think so? I *have* been going to Zumba classes and I think my arms are getting stronger." I flex, showing off the little bulging bicep that I've been working on. It took a lot of fist pumps to eighties rock to grow it, so I'm pretty proud.

"Nice!" Chris exclaims. "Alright, want to get me out of these?" He moves his arms a little bit.

I reach past the neckline of my dress, into my bra, and start fishing around for the little silver key.

As I'm searching, Chris's radio cackles to life. I recognize the voice of Ted McDougal, Chris's partner, speaking in a business-like tone. "616 to 618, I'm tied up with a parking meter dispute on Aspen, and just got report of a dog that got out of his leash in front of the library. Could you head in that direction?"

Chris frowns. "Uh oh," he says.

I'm still searching. My fingertips have not hit any metal. Plus, I'm noticing how loose the bra fits. I always tuck money into my bra, because sometimes it's nice not to carry my wallet around. I've never lost anything before. But I've never worn a bra this loose-fitting before, either.

"Penny, why are you reaching into your dress like that?" Chris asks. "The key is in your *pocket*, right?"

"I don't have pockets in this dress," I say. "My bra is like my pocket. I always put stuff in my bra. It's just --"

"You put the key into your bra?" Chris repeats.

"Yes. I've never lost anything before," I say. "Only all of my underwear that actually fit are in the washing machine, because I did a mega-load of laundry this morning. So what I'm wearing is from years back, when I was a few pounds heavier, and..."

"What are you saying?" Chris asks.

"I'm saying, it might have fallen out," I say. "This bra is too big. I think the key just slipped out to the ground. I'll just poke around for a minute and --"

The radio interrupts my statement. "616 to 618?" the officer says.

"That's McDougal," Chris says. "Damn. Okay, Penny, hold that radio up to my face, okay?"

I stop searching the ground for the key, and do as Chris says. When it's in front of his face, he tells me to press the button on the side. As I press it, he says, "618 to 616. I'm up Mill Creek road and I'm detained for the time being. Go ahead and call that one into animal control."

"Copy that," Ted says. "I already did call it in, but Marty's taking an early lunch."

Chris shakes his head. After thinking for a minute, he says. "Ten four. I'll be there as soon as possible. Just let me finish up this little bit of business up here on Mill Creek."

"Copy," Ted says.

I push the radio back into Chris's holster, and then begin searching the ground furiously. Chris helps. Together we go over every inch of the flattened grass where we've been playing.

It's easy for me, since I can work on my hands and knees, combing the grass. Chris, however, can't use his hands. He's parting the grass with his feet, and hunched over almost double. Even with both of us searching, after twenty minutes we've got nothing.

"Where could it be?" Chris says, clearly frustrated.

"I don't know!" I feel horrible. This is my fault! "Maybe I should drive us back to town, and we could borrow some metal cutters."

"*You* drive the cop car back to town while *I* ride along handcuffed?" Chris asks, horrified. "What would my chief say?"

"I don't know!" I say. "But it's better than doing nothing! What if there's an emergency? What if Ted really needs you -- for something other than a runaway dog? You're on duty, Chris!"

"This is bad," Chris says, as if the severity is just now hitting him. "Really, really bad."

"Maybe it got caught in my dress," I say, running my hands over the front of my outfit. The knit pattern is full of little ridges and bumps. It's impossible to tell if I'm feeling a thin metal key or not.

"Hang on," I say, as I begin pulling the dress up off my head.

"What are you doing?" Chris asks.

I pull the dress completely off me, and then lie it, inside out, on the grass in front of me. "This is the only way I can see -- oh! Oh my goodness!" I'm so relieved, I'm shouting. "Chris! It's right here! It got caught in the dress; it didn't even make it to the ground!"

I'm on all fours, in just my bra and underwear, plus my Power Spell necklace, when the sound of a vehicle approaching -- fast -- cuts through the air.

It's a police car.

The *Chiefs* police car, to be exact. I stand up, reach for my dress as fast as I can.

It's not fast enough.

Just as soon as I stand, the police Chief gets out of his car.

Chris looks mortified.

I feel like I want to crawl into a hole and die. It's not that I care what the Chief thinks of me. The police chief already doesn't like me, and I got over it a long time ago.

But he is Chris's boss, and this does *not* look good.

Not at all.

For an instant, I freeze. Then, I fumble with my dress and manage to get it over my head. The key is still in my hand and I walk over to Chris. The handcuffs spring off Chris just as the Chief walks up to us.

"This... doesn't look good, does it, Chief Holcomb?" Chris asks.

The chief shakes his head. "I heard your radio traffic. Wondered to myself what you were doing up on Mill Creek road. Your GPS showed that you've been up here for an hour and a half."

"I was giving Penny a lesson on temporary restrains," Chris says, somberly.

The chief squints at me. "And she... had to take her dress off, for that lesson?" he asks.

"No, Chief, sir," Chris says, stuttering a little as he speaks. "No, that was to find the key. To the handcuffs. It was lost ... inside of her dress."

"It snagged on the knitting," I say. "All of those little loops of yarn..." I laugh nervously. "We found it though." I hold the key up, and the now open handcuffs. "Hooray!" I say, weakly.

The chief says nothing. He continues to eye us. Then, he turns on his heel. As he walks away, he calls out, "Christopher, stop by my office when you get back to town."

I look at Chris. His shoulders slump.

The chief pulls away.

"I'm sorry," I mumble to Chris, as the dust clears.

"It's not your fault," he says. Then, thinking, he says, "Well, it kind of is. Who doesn't carry a set of keys with them?"

I don't offer an answer. I'm too embarrassed.

The drive down Mill Creek road is a long, quiet one.

When Chris drops me at my bike, I give him a little peck on the cheek. "Good luck at your meeting with the Chief," I say.

"Thanks," he mumbles.

I grab my glasses off of the dashboard and then my bag from the back seat, and get out. Once on the sidewalk, I stand and watch as Chris pulls away. Then I push the handcuffs I've been holding into my bag, and pull out my phone so that I can check the time.

It's already twelve.

Hopefully, my afternoon is going to be better than my morning.

Chapter Seven

Marley is laughing so hard, I'm afraid some of her Funky Buddha drink is going to spray out of her nose, all over the steering wheel of her van. I have reason to be wary -- it's happened before.

"It's not funny!" I say. "I think Chris is in a lot of trouble. He shouldn't have been out there."

"Locked in handcuffs...." She's trying to breathe but failing. Her face is turning a surprising shade of red, given her Native American heritage. "...With you... in your underwear!"

It's a good thing she's not driving. We'd be off the road right now, in a ditch. There are little tears beading up around her eyes. She squeezes her eyes shut as she wipes the tears away.

"Marley!" I say, sharply. "I can't laugh about this!" My lip wiggles. Is a smile breaking out on my face? I look out the passenger window to hide it from her.

I guess it's true what they say, about laughter being contagious. I'm exposed, and the condition is catching.

I turn back to my friend, trying to keep a straight face. "He *shouldn't* have been up there!" I say. "It was my stupid idea. Now he has to meet with his boss. All because I --"

"*Handcuffed* your police officer boyfriend and *lost* the key."

An uninvited spurt of laughter escapes from my lips. As I laugh my glasses start sliding down my nose. It feels good to push them back up. Maybe all that nonsense up on Mill Creek happened because I wasn't wearing the glasses. Would a brainy, brilliant PI choose to store a small, thin key inside of baggy, stretchy undergarments, for safekeeping?

I think not.

I make a mental note to wear the glasses from sunup to sundown, in the future. Maybe that way I'll be able to avoid embarrassing situations like this.

Once Marley and I wind up our laughing fit, she says, "So what are you going to ask Ralph, once we spot him?"

We've been sitting in Marley's van for fifteen minutes now, in the alley behind The Place. It's about two. I've already run all my errands, minus the grocery shopping. So, basically, I just delivered my rent to Sherry. Well, she wasn't there, so I slid the packet of money under her office door.

Immediately after it disappeared under the crack, I had regrets. Was it wise to push all of that cash under a door? What if someone else spotted it, or a mouse scurried off with it? There are plenty of mice in the old Nugget building.

To rectify the situation, I called her cellphone to tell her that the money was waiting for her. Her voicemail message informed me that she was out of town, camping in the desert for the week, which didn't ease my worries.

However, what was done was done. I couldn't very well get the money back through the narrow crack, unless I used a coat hanger and maybe some tape or tongs of some sort (which did cross my mind, I have to admit).

Marley had also run all of her errands, and wanted to help me track down Ralph. After cruising the town for a while, listening to Hillcrest's only radio station, we settled on parking in front of the restaurant.

I reasoned that since Ralph now owned The Place, he'd likely turn up for work eventually. Marley reasoned that sitting parked would save some gas money.

"I'm going to get Ralph talking about Joe, I suppose," I say. "I want to see what his energy is like. You know, does he get all nervous or upset or anything."

"Melanie got pretty nervous or upset when you talked about Joe," Marley says. "But that doesn't mean she killed him."

"I know," I say. "But that's the best way to start… just ease into things. I'll ask him a couple questions about that day at the restaurant, and just see how he reacts. Then I might try to lead into some questions about Melanie. I'm still trying to figure out how her tickets to Oahu fit in with all of this."

"That *is* what Mayor Haywater hired you for," Marley reminds me.

As if I need reminding.

I'm well aware that I'll need to call Cliff with an update soon, as I promised. I'm not sure that I've gotten anywhere, except for hearing the rumor that his wife was going to ask for a divorce. I sure as heck am not going to drop that little bomb into his lap without concrete evidence. And even if I do get solid evidence, the conversation is *not* going to be fun.

I'm dreading it actually.

"Ooo!" Marley says, after a long sip of her soy chai latte with a quad shot of espresso. "I just got an idea!"

It's like the espresso has switched on a lightbulb inside of her head. Her eyes open wide and she starts waving one hand around in that way she does when she's excited. "We could do a good cop-bad cop thing! You could be the good cop, and I could be the bad cop! It would be like in the movies -- you know when one of them is all compassionate and sweet, and then BAM! The other one hits the perp with a question."

"First of all," I say, straightening my glasses. "We're not cops. I'm a PI, and you work part time as a massage therapist. Secondly, Ralph isn't a 'perp'. He's a suspect."

Marley sips her Funky Buddha. She's not happy with my reality check.

"I like your enthusiasm, though," I add. Because I'm curious, I ask, "Do you even know what a perp is?"

I don't get to find out her answer, because just then I spot Ralph, walking down the alley towards us.

"There he is!" I say.

Ralph is a short man. Usually, whenever I see him, he's trailing after Mayor Haywater. Up until recently,

Ralph helped Cliff manage two businesses and mayoral duties. Now that Ralph owns the town's busiest restaurant, I wonder if he'll still function as an assistant to Cliff. I doubt it.

It's odd seeing him on his own, without Cliff.

He's wearing pressed khakis, a crisp white tee-shirt, and a black blazer, unbuttoned. Aviator glasses and gelled hair finish off his stylish look.

"I don't remember Ralph dressing up like this," I say. "He looks all styled out. Has he always dressed like he's heading to a photoshoot of GQ magazine? Maybe I just never looked at his clothing before."

Marley shakes her head. "You're right," she says. "He used to wear frumpy clothes, before he bought the restaurant. I think he went shopping. New job, new wardrobe, I suppose."

"He looks pretty pleased with himself," I say, as Ralph saunters up to the back door of The Place.

I step out of the van and slam the door close just as Ralph is about to disappear into the restaurant. He turns and looks at me.

"Ralph!" I call out. "Hi! Could we have a word with you?"

He grins. His grin widens as Marley steps out of the van, too. Maybe he thinks we're restaurant-owner groupies or something, I don't know. I *do* know that I don't like the sleazy look he's giving us, and I'm eager to set him straight.

But before I can introduce the purpose of our visit, he speaks. "Hello, ladies! To what do I owe the pleasure?" He runs one hand through his slick hair and then tilts his glasses down and looks us over.

I hate to burst his bubble. Then again, he's kind of giving me the creeps, so maybe it's not so bad.

"I'm a private investigator," I say.

"Right," he replies, slowly. His demeanor changes a little bit. "I've heard you do that… you're Penny Banks, right?"

"Yes," I say. "And this is my friend, Marley."

"How is business?" Ralph asks. "That must be a tough job to hold down in a small town like this. Not much crime in Hillcrest." He laughs, but it's a fake laugh.

"Oh, you'd be surprised," I say.

"She figured out who was stealing the Payday candy bars from the Market," Marley says.

Ralph scoffs. "Anyone could have done that," he says. "I'm guessing it was the checkout woman, who kept gaining weight. What was her name… Marge? She always had chocolate smudges on her cheeks." He laughs. "Once I saw her actually take a candy bar off the shelf and eat it while she was ringing up my food."

Shoot. He's right. It was Marge. Was it really that obvious?

"Well, *I* didn't see that, and I still figured it out," I say.

"What is your point?" asks Ralph.

Crap. What *is* my point?

"Where were you on the day that Joe Gallant was murdered?" Marley asks, in a demanding voice.

Ralph looks as though he's just been delivered a right hook to the face. He jerks his head back, and then does a double take, looking from Marley to me.

"M- Murdered?" he says. "Joe wasn't murdered. He got stuck."

"I didn't ask for your opinion," Marley says. "I asked you where you were."

"I -- I was here," he says, with a slight stutter.

Nice one, Marley.

Playing good cop, I say, "We just want to ask you a few questions, Ralph. Would that be okay with you?"

He's still off balance. I can tell he wants to refuse, but his brain is still scrambled from Marley's abrupt question and aggressive demeanor.

"Did you kill Joe Gallant, by stuffing him into the deep freezer?" Marley asks.

Ralph takes a step back, away from us. "What! I didn't kill Joe!" he says, too loud. He's nervous.

Then again, who wouldn't be when accused of murder!?

I feel like we need to reel things in. I guess that's where the good cop comes in.

"Ralph," I say, in a quiet, calm voice. "We're trying to gather some information about Joe's death. It would be very helpful if we could run some timelines by you -- just to verify what other people have told us. It won't take long."

He still seems undecided about whether he wants to talk to us or not. We can't force him to, so I keep talking. I am hoping that if I keep his attention, he won't just disappear through the restaurant doors. "On the day that Joe was found dead in the freezer, you were seen entering the restaurant at eleven in the morning. Is that correct?"

"Cliff asked me to do some work here," Ralph says. "He was tied up with the retirement party, but he knew there would be a full house at the restaurant that night."

"Because it was his last night as the owner," I say.

"Yeah," Ralph says. "We knew the whole town would be coming in for dinner. Though I don't know what the big deal is. I haven't changed anything on the menu."

"How is it, owning a restaurant?" I ask. "Do you like it?" As the good cop, I care about Ralph's feelings. I know Marley will chime in with some hard-core questions soon, so I can afford to putter around with the soft stuff. "It must be nice," I add. "This is such a popular place." I decide to really butter him up. "I've heard that it's even better now that you're the owner."

"Really?" Ralph says. "Who said that?"

"Oh, just people… around town. The word is that the food tastes fresher."

"I did replace the bulb in one of our warming lights," Ralph says. "Now when Glenn puts food up there, it stays a lot hotter. I wonder if that's what people are tasting."

"Must be," I say. "Is Glenn doing most of the cooking… now that Joe is gone?" I ask.

"I promoted him to head chef," Ralph says. "He already knows the menu. It was a natural choice-- "

"For an astute business leader like yourself," I say.

He actually smiles. This is working!

Marley chimes in. "What did you do, when you entered the restaurant at eleven am on August fourteenth?" she demands.

Ralph is once again shaken. He looks over at Marley warily as he answers. "I went straight to Cliff's office."

"Did you see Joe, working in the kitchen?" I ask.

"No," Ralph says. "I assumed he was there, doing prep work. I heard Glenn come in an hour later. I didn't go into the kitchen. I was in the office, doing administrative work. I didn't come out of the office until hours later, when the paramedics arrived and pronounced Joe dead."

"You expect us to believe that?" Marley practically shouts, causing Ralph to flinch. She glares at Ralph, as she repeats his words back to him. Every once in a while, at random, she throws in air quotes. "Oh, you assumed Joe was 'in' the kitchen, and you heard 'Glenn' come in, hm? And you just hid away in your office until hours 'later'. Yeah right."

The air quotes seem totally random. I'm going to have to give her a lesson in using them, if we're going to do this routine again, because as it is she's almost making me laugh aloud. I am the nice cop, but I'm not the giggly cop. That would be over the top.

Ralph is confused. "That's what I said," He says, giving Marley a weird look.

For the first time, Marley is flustered. "Yeah, well..." she says.

I jump in. "What my friend here is saying is that we're going to need some proof that you were in Cliff's office while Joe was freezing to death. Can you tell us about the work that you were doing?"

His face flushes a little bit. "Why would I remember that?" He asks. "I did office work for Cliff all the time, before I bought this restaurant. A *lot* of work. I was probably making phone calls. He was expecting inventory to be delivered, and I was the one who had to receive everything and make payments."

"Can you verify that for us somehow?" I ask. "Maybe show us some of the receipts from that day, and provide a log of calls that you made so that we can --"

"I don't have to prove anything to you," Ralph says.

Shoot. He just caught on to the fact that we have absolutely zero authority in this matter.

I cringe.

He catches it. "Actually," he says, "I don't even have to *talk* to you. You're not the police."

"Like I said, I'm a private investigator," I say.

"And who hired you?" Ralph asks.

"That's confidential," I say. I can sense we're going to lose him soon. "Ralph, I've heard you don't get along well with Melanie Haywater. Tell us about your relationship with her."

This puts him over the edge. "That's *enough*," he says. "I have a restaurant to run. I don't have time for this."

He spins on his heel, and disappears through the restaurant's back door. Once he's inside, he slams the door closed.

It clearly says employees only. We can't follow him inside. It's after two, so the restaurant is open. But I have a feeling that even if we went around to the front and entered the restaurant as customers, Ralph would avoid us like the plague.

I'm thinking over what he's just told us. "According to Ralph, Glenn was alone in the kitchen with Joe for hours before Cliff came in at two thirty," I say, thinking aloud.

"Plenty of time to stuff him in a freezer," Marley says. "Glenn had the opportunity."

"And the motive," I say. "He might have wanted to become head chef. I bet he got a pay raise."

"Means and motive," Marley says. She's hung out with me enough to pick up on some PI lingo. We start walking back to the van.

As we climb in, I say, "I guess we should talk to Glenn, next."

"Sounds like it," Marley agrees. "You make a stellar good cop, by the way."

"And you're a decent bad cop," I say.

"Just decent?" she asks.

"We have to work on your use of air quotes," I say.

"Yeah, that didn't feel right." She pulls the van out of the alleyway, back onto the main street.

"Do you believe everything Ralph just said?" she asks.

"I don't know," I answer. It's not the answer I *want* to give, but it's the truth. I'd much rather say, 'heck, no,' or 'absolutely', but I have no clear feeling on the matter.

Is Ralph telling us the truth? I wish I knew.

Absentmindedly, I reach for the pouch that's hanging around my neck. I hold onto it as I wish for better instincts. No luck.

Marley sees me holding the pouch. "Have you figured out your secret key ingredient?" she asks, as she steers the van down the main street.

"Nope," I say. "How about you?"

She thinks for a minute. "Well, last night I poured a glass of chardonnay, and I kind of wondered -- what if chardonnay is my secret ingredient? I've heard that I'm friendlier after I've had a glass."

"I don't know if friendlier really has anything to do with the power spell."

"Yeah, I guess," Marley says. "What about cinnamon... do you think that could be it? I really like putting cinnamon on everything I eat. Even waffles."

"Does it make you feel powerful?" I ask.

She shakes her head.

"I think you have to keep waiting. I feel like when we really find the secret key ingredient, we're going to know."

"Bummer," Marley says. "I was really hoping mine would be one of those. Do you have a Book of Shadows? The spell instructions say that we have to write down what we figure out in our Book of Shadows. I don't have one."

"Me either." I say.

"Maybe the pharmacy has some blank journals," Marley says. We've reached the turn to Blackbear apartments, and Marley slows the van down, stopping traffic behind us.

"Should I drop you home?" she asks.

"Yeah, thanks," I say. "I promised myself I'd go to the grocery store today. Maybe I'll sneak in a trip before Chris gets home from work. We're supposed to hang out tonight."

Marley steers the van down the road to my apartment.

"Maybe *your* secret key ingredient is Chris," she suggests.

"I doubt it," I say. "I was wearing my necklace today while he was training me with the handcuffs. When the chief pulled up and I was practically naked, I definitely didn't feel powerful. *Mortified* would be a better word for what I felt. Now, if we were looking for a secret ingredient to an embarrassment spell, Chris would be my ticket."

Marley laughs.

Before getting out of the van, I reach across the console and give her a hug. "Thanks," I say.

"We didn't make much progress," Marley says, as we pull apart.

"These things take time," I say. "We're getting closer; slowly but surely." I hop out and slam the door closed.

As Marley pulls off, I give her a wave. Then, when she's gone, I turn and begin walking towards my apartment. As I pass by Unit B, I look for signs of life. According to Cora, someone signed a lease to live there. I wonder who?

Once I'm on the staircase that leads to my apartment, my mind returns to the case.

I was trying to sound optimistic for Marley, but really I'm feeling anything but. The interview with Ralph did little but add to my confusion.

Instead of answers, I have more questions. What seemed to be simply a case about a mysterious plane ticket is becoming more and more complex. Not only that, but I feel like with every step I take, I'm getting farther from the issue of Melanie's travel itinerary.

At least I can hope that at any moment, I'll be gifted with some sort of magical superpowers, due to the satchel of ingredients around my neck. I place my palm around the little pouch and give it a squeeze as I climb my stairs. I feel the lump of ingredients shift within the old curtain material.

This is the kind of necklace I might expect a woman in an insane asylum to wear.

But I'm not crazy.

Am I?

Chapter Eight

I bend over and push half a gallon of soy milk into the fridge, next to a carton of vanilla soy coffee creamer and a six pack of beer.

I'd like to say that I have to scooch aside copious fruits and vegetables to make way for the soy milk, but I don't. My fridge remains typically sparse, despite the trip to the Hillcrest Market that I just took.

That's not entirely due to my lack of skill in the kitchen, or my lack of imagination when it comes to preparing meals. It's more due to the fact that I can only fit so much in the milk crate that is strapped to the back of my bike.

If I'd been driving a car, sure, I would have loaded up the trunk with stalks of celery and buckets of healthy, leafy greens.

That's my story, and I'm sticking to it.

I straighten up and put the nearly empty paper bag on the countertop. There's one more thing inside of it: a blank composition book, that I bought at the market.

It's nothing fancy, but I think it will be just fine as my Book of Shadows for right now. I pull it out of the bag and place it reverently on the countertop, pleased with myself for purchasing it. I have to move aside a bunch of bananas to flip open the book. Though my fridge certainly isn't packed with fruits and veggies, at least I bought bananas. Go me!

Grabbing a pen, I begin writing on the first blank page of the composition book: *'This is Witch Penny Bank's Book of Shadows'*.

I pause and take a look at my work.

It feels strange to see the word 'witch' next to my name, but it also feels… exciting.

I'm so absorbed in gazing at the words that I startle when there's a knock at the door.

I flip the book close, put the pen down, and make my way over. It's a short walk, since my apartment's little kitchen is practically right in the entryway.

I pull the door open.

Chris is standing there, with a box of pizza and a six pack of beer. He's freshly showered, dressed in his usual shorts and tee.

I smile, stand on my tiptoes, and give him a quick kiss. "Did you get out twenty minutes ago?" I ask.

"Eighteen," he says.

"Speed demon!" I say, laughing as I reach for the pizza. I spin around and set it on the counter. "You must be getting close to beating the record for the world's fastest shower."

"Nope," Chris says. "I heard that's locked in at thirty-six point one seconds. I'm nowhere near there."

I laugh again. "How do you know that?" I ask, as Chris follows me in and closes the door behind him. He places the beers on the countertop, next to the pizza.

"A geeky girl told me," he says, grinning as he pops the top of two beers.

"Who?" I ask.

He steps in closer to me and gives me a kiss on the cheek before handing me the open beer. "*You* did, Penny. Last year," he laughs. "Don't you remember?"

I shake my head. I *am* geeky, but I don't remember saying that. "You have a good memory," I note.

"When it comes to *you*, I do," Chris says.

I sip my beer, and then look up at him through my lashes. He's still staring at me. I like it when he looks at me like this.

We just look at each other for a minute. It's nice.

Then I ask, "How did it go with the Chief? Did you two have a talk?"

This breaks the spell. Chris reaches for one of the tattered bar stools that I have positioned around the countertop (I really need to cover those, soon!), and then takes a seat. He sips his beer before answering.

I still haven't run the dishwasher, so I reach for paper towels.

Chris accepts one. "Chief gave me a lecture about appropriate behavior when on duty," he says, reaching for the pizza box. "It was pretty much what I expected. All the guys think we were *doing things* in the field." Chris chuckles, and glances up at me. "They want me to give them advice… you know, for in the bedroom."

I'm blushing now. "Just because I wasn't dressed and you were in handcuffs doesn't mean--",I stop short, and laugh. "It does sound bad, doesn't it?"

"Especially to those guys. I swear, sometimes it's hard to say anything around the station, without getting ragged on. Those guys have minds in the gutter. It's like they're always thinking about… you know."

I know.

Now *my* mind is in the gutter.

See, when Chris and I first dated, five years ago, things got hot and heavy really, really fast.

Embarrassingly fast.

As in, I don't even want to admit how fast things went.

A few months into our whirlwind affair, I was struggling in academy, and then I got kicked out. Chris broke up with me soon after. So this time, we've been taking things slow.

Really slow.

It's been months, and we've kept it to kissing.

Now, standing here in the kitchen and talking with Chris about bedroom activities… that's all I can think about.

I'm pretty sure he's thinking along the same lines, because now when our eyes meet, this sizzling tension passes between us.

Shoot.

Must. Take. This. Slow.

Brakes! I need to hit the brakes.

I break eye contact and reach for a slice of pizza. I put it down on my paper towel.

"Okay, so we're going to have to live with some jokes for a while," I say.

"I don't know if the guys are *ever* going to let go of this one," Chris says with a laugh. "It is pretty funny."

"Yeah," I say. "I can't believe that happened. You know when you were handing me the box, with the key in it?" I say.

"Yeah?" Chris says. "You looked kind of scared."

"That's because I thought it might be an engagement ring!" I say, lifting my eyebrows. "Now *that* would be crazy!"

"Crazy?" Chris's smile fades

"Yeah. Pretty ridiculous, hm?" I try to keep my voice light. I know I'm steering us into choppy waters, but I can't stop myself.

Maybe this is my way of putting on the brakes.

"I mean," I say, avoiding Chris's eyes. "We've only been dating for a few months, and it's not even like we're *seriously* dating. This is all pretty casual."

Chris says nothing to this.

The sizzling tension between us goes flat.

Yep! Success. The brakes are now on full bore, screeching us to a halt. I may have even stopped the momentum so completely that we're now moving in the other direction.

"Yeah, we're keeping things casual, because that's what you wanted," Chris says. "At least, that's what I *think* you want. We never really talk about this kind of thing, Penny."

"That's because we're not good at talking about it," I say. Ug. This is painful.

"Well, maybe we're going to have to get better at it. If we're going to make this work," Chris says.

If? What does he mean, 'if' we're going to make this work?

Chris just *admitted* that this might not work! That means another break-up. Am I going to survive that kind of heartbreak, a second time?

I remember how lost I felt. How alone.

I can't go there again.

Chris has stopped eating. I can't even look at my pizza. I have no appetite.

I really hate conversations like this. I can tell that Chris does too.

When he speaks, his voice is strained. "How do you think this is going, between us?" he asks.

"Good," I say. "Great."

"Then why did you make a face like I was handing you a ticking time bomb when you thought I might be proposing?" he asks. "Because one day, I might propose to you, Penny. If that ever happens, I'd hope that you would feel... I don't know... excited? Happy?"

"Yeah, but Chris, that's years down the road. We've only been dating for a few months. It's way too early to --"

"We've been in a relationship for more than five years, Penny," Chris says.

"That's not true," I argue. "We were doing *something* -- sleeping together, I guess -- and then we broke up. *That* was five years ago. Things ended, pretty badly."

"Okay... maybe our history isn't perfect," Chris says. "You might not see a story like ours on the Hallmark movie channel. But it's still *our* story, Penny. I like it.

We've been through alot. And even when we weren't together, we were still neighbors."

"Yeah, but you were dating Nathalie."

He nods. "Okay. True enough. But Penny... that whole time, I knew that I wanted to be with you again. I just didn't know when, or how. I never stopped caring about you."

"That was a weird way to show you cared about me," I say, bitterly. "Don't you think, Chris? Spending all of your time with another woman?"

"This isn't about me and Nathalie!" Chris says. "This is about me and you! I don't know how we're going to move forward if you can't get over the fact that I dated Nathalie."

"I don't either," I say, honestly. There's a lump in my throat now. I know I'm being dramatic, but I truly feel like I might cry.

Being with Chris scares me. I'm petrified of finding myself back in that place where he's my whole world. Then, if he ends things again, I'll be back at rock bottom. I'll have to build my life up again. It's better if I just don't allow myself to become so utterly dependent on him again.

An uncomfortable silence is unfolding between us.

Neither of us is eating, or drinking.

The melting pizza cheese that has spilled from the slice and onto the paper towel is now congealed and fused to the paper. It looks totally unappetizing. Even if I did try to eat, I have a feeling that the food would just get stuck in the giant lump that's sitting in my throat.

"Maybe I just need some time to think about this," I say, quietly.

Chris blows out some air, and then pushes his beer and pizza away.

He gets up, off his stool.

"I'll leave you to it," he says flatly.

I look at his barely touched slice, and his half full beer. "What will you have for dinner?" I ask.

"I'll find something," he says.

He walks over to me, and plants a kiss on my forehead. I stand perfectly still. I feel frozen. I don't even turn as he makes his way to the door.

"Good night, Penny," he says.

"Good night, Chris," I manage.

I hear the door click closed.

Why am I pushing him away like this? I know that I'm scared of being hurt again, but is my fear really that big?

I could get over it, if I tried.

I could let myself fall for him again, if it wasn't for a deeper fear that I can now feel, stirring inside of me.

It's one that I'm barely able to name, let alone face.

I've *changed*.

I'm becoming a witch.

What if Chris doesn't like the woman I'm on my way to becoming?

This thought terrifies me.

Chapter Nine

I reach for the pizza slice in front of me, which is now glued with congealed cheese to the paper napkin beneath it, and pick it up. It feels strangely satisfying to throw the whole thing into the trash can. I scoop up Chris' partially eaten slice and add it to the receptacle as well.

In a way, it feels like I'm erasing the conversation that just occurred, though I know that's impossible.

I'm about to clean up the beer bottles, but I stop short when I hear a knock on my door.

Is it Chris?

Maybe he's figured out something to say that will take away this lump from my throat, and this fear from the pit of my stomach.

Maybe he'll hold me and kiss me and make it all feel better.

I open the door with a sense of hope, and I can't help it that my face falls when I see Cora standing there.

"Don't look so excited to see me," she says sarcastically.

"Sorry," I make way for her, and she walks past me, into the apartment.

I follow her. "I thought it might be Chris. We just had a rough conversation. He left but I thought he was coming back. Did you see him out there?"

Cora shakes her head. "Are you fighting?" she asks.

"No -- not exactly. It's just something happened today, and we were trying to talk about it but--"

"Oh… the handcuff thing? I heard about that. Only you, Penny. Only you." She shakes her head while laughing.

"That could have happened to anybody," I say.

"No," she says. "It really couldn't."

Our talking has stirred Turkey, and he comes over to greet us.

"What couldn't have happened to anybody but you?" he asks, silently. "What is it this time?"

"It's a long story," I answer, telepathically. "I'll tell you later."

Or, maybe I won't.

"How about some dinner?" Turkey asks.

I begin walking to the pantry, to grab his cat food. As I walk, I talk to Cora. "Do you carry keys with you?" I ask.

"Always," Cora says, lifting a set of keys and jingling them in the air. "They're for my car, my house, and the office."

"Your office door locks?" I say.

Hm. Maybe part of adulting is having an office door that locks. Since I work from a supply closet with a rickety door that barely *closes*, let alone locks, I wouldn't know.

I lift Turkey's dish, place it on the counter, and begin filling it with dry cat food.

"Of course it locks," she says. Then, she eyes the inside of the pantry. I left the door open after getting Turkey's food, and she has a clear line of site into my cereal collection.

"Do you *live* on sugary cereal?" she asks.

"No," I say. Then, to deflect the focus from my poor eating habits, I ask, "What brings you over, Cora?"

She hops up onto a bar stool, her shiny blond ponytail bouncing. "I found something out. I thought it might help you with the investigative work you're doing for the mayor."

"Great," I say. "What is it?"

"Okay," Cora says, placing her hands down on the countertops. "You're going to love me for this or hate me, I'm not quite sure."

"I already love you," I say. "I'm not going to hate you. Go ahead. What is it?"

"Melanie was *definitely* planning to file for a divorce. I found out today. I happened to be sorting through some of Hiroku's documents, and..." she shrugs, innocently. "Sometimes you see things, right? Hiroku drafted the petition for dissolution of marriage for Melanie Haywater."

"You're talking in Lawyer Speak," I say. "What does that mean?"

"It's just divorce papers. Hiroku writes up the petition, and then Melanie was basically supposed to hire someone to serve the papers to Cliff. Everything was all set on Hiroku's side, and Melanie was going to serve the papers on August fourteenth, but she called it off."

"She didn't go through with it?" I ask

Cora shakes her head.

I put a dollop of Finicky Feline Feast wet food on top of the heap of dry, and then place the dish on the floor.

"You didn't hear it from me," Cora says happily, as she slides off her stool.

I swear, there is nothing this woman enjoys more than gossip. I wonder if Hiroku knows that she has a leak the size of a pipeline in her law office. The word 'confidential' is not in Cora's vocabulary.

If I had a secret, I'd rather publish it on Wikipedia than tell Cora about it.

"Well, I've gotta run," she says. "I'm going to go home and whip up a healthy dinner. I'm thinking a big salad with some lean chicken breast on it."

See? Pure adult. Through and through. Maybe I should be taking notes.

"Okay," I say, seeing my friend to the door. I hold it open for her. "Thanks for stopping by. That's helpful information."

"I thought so," she says. "I wanted to tell you in person instead of emailing or calling. Who knows whose monitoring that stuff, these days. I know I'm not supposed to tell you this private stuff from work, but if it can help you figure out who killed Joe, it's important."

Okay, maybe she has more of a conscience than I've given her credit for.

Before she turns to head down the hallway, I ask, "Have you had any luck with figuring out your secret key ingredient?"

She shakes her head. "Nothing yet. But I am wearing my satchel." She pulls her necklace from beneath her blouse. "It's nearly *killing* me," she adds, with a heavy sigh, "But I'm doing it."

I laugh, and we say goodbye. She's a few steps from the walkway when she turns back. She's pulling something from her purse.

"I almost forgot!" she says, retracing her steps. "My boss, Hiroku, is looking for a nanny for her Chihuahua. I thought of you, because she's going to pay one hundred bucks a week. You're always stressed about your office rent, so…" she hands me the card.

I see 'Hiroku Itsu: Lawyer' emblazoned on it, and also a phone number and email address.

"Give her a call," Cora says, as I read. "She already said she would hire you."

"A nanny… for her *Chihuahua*?" I repeat.

Cora shrugs. "Her dog is super high maintenance, but it wouldn't be that bad."

"I'll think about it," I say.

Once I close the door, I'm excited and agitated. I stuff the card into my wallet, along with Cliff's. I'm not going to be a dog's nanny. My office rent is paid for the month, thanks to Cliff, and I really need to dedicate my time to my investigative work. That's what Cliff is paying me for, and Chihuahua-sitting would only be a distraction.

My mind is whirring over the news that Cora has just shared.

Melanie was going to file for a divorce, on August fourteenth -- the *day* that Joe died.

Another coincidence?

I don't think so.

Her divorce papers could have something to do with Joe's death, and her trip to Hawaii.

I really need to call Cliff and give him an update, but what on earth am I going to tell him?

Now that I know Melanie was planning on filing for divorce, I'm realizing what a sticky situation I am in. A sticky, *sad* situation. Plus, I'm not even supposed to *know* about the divorce papers.

Sheesh.

"Why are you pacing?" Turkey asks. He's finished with his dinner and is sitting on a bar stool looking at me.

"Am I pacing?" I respond.

Yep. I sure am. I stop in my tracks. "I feel like I have to *do* something," I tell my cat. "I can't just sit here in this apartment while this case is so far from solved."

"You just don't want to sit here and mope over your fight with Chris," Turkey says.

"It wasn't a fight!" I retort.

He stares me down, until I admit, "Fine I guess it was a fight. And yes, I wouldn't mind a little distraction from that. It won't do me any good to sit here and feel sorry for myself. Work will take my mind off of things."

I start pacing again.

"Wearing a track in the carpet isn't going to help you figure out who killed Joe," Turkey says.

"You're right, Turkey." I walk over to him and give him a few pets on the top of his head.

"As usual," he says, before starting to purr. I pet him for a few more minutes, while thinking about what I can do to make some progress. Then, mid-stroke, I get an idea. I pull my hand away from Turkey's head.

"That's it!" I whisper.

"What?" Turkey asks. He looks peeved that I stopped petting him, but curious at the same time. I know, that's a lot to get from a cat expression, but I know my cat well. I can read the curl of his lip and the tilt of his little whisker-spiked eyebrows.

"I'll go to the OP," I say. "Glenn's usually there, having a drink after he finishes his shift at The Place. I'll pretend that I'm there to drink. Heck, maybe I'll have a glass of wine --"

"Just *one*," says Turkey sternly.

"Or two," I say. "And I'll see if I can get some information out of him. I think he might open up to me more if I'm not talking to him as a private investigator. It'll just be a friendly conversation between two people hanging out at a bar..."

"Be careful," Turkey says, as I grab my messenger bag and head for the door. "He could be a killer."

With that in mind, I head out into the night.

******

It's *never* a good idea for me to have wine on an empty stomach.

The alcohol goes straight to my head, and soon I have a very unprofessional head-buzz going on.

Glenn isn't even here, but I'm determined to wait for him until he arrives. I'm sure he's going to enter the bar, sooner or later. He's a staple here.

"Can I get you another?" the bartender, Janine asks, as I polish off the last drops of white wine from my glass.

I scan the bar for Glenn. Still not here. "Sure," I say.

"You are waiting on Chris, hon?" Janine asks me.

"No," I say.

"You're here by yourself?" She uncorks the bottle of house white and begins refilling my glass.

"Yep," I answer, while tapping my toe idly to the country music that's playing in the background. "Just me, out by myself, having a glass of wine."

Just then, I hear a deep, familiar voice, on my right. "Then is it alright if I sit here?"

I turn.

My cheeks flush, immediately. Why does blood always rush to my face the instant I see Doctor Maxwell Shire?

"Uh… yeah… sure, you can sit there," I say awkwardly, while Janine delivers my drink.

She quickly takes Max's order, and then steps away. I wish she'd stay.

I don't feel like I'm in the right frame of mind to be on my own with a vampire.

He grins at me. His eyes and teeth, sparkling white, reflect the bar lights above with a little twinkle. Is it strange that even his fangs look attractive to me right now? I must have more of a wine-buzz going on than I thought.

Feeling a bit faint, I push the second glass away from me so that I don't drink it too fast, due to my nerves. Instead, I reach for the food menu.

The OP has extremely limited food options. Basically, there's only three things on it: a small serving of gravy fries, a medium serving of gravy fries, or a large serving of gravy fries.

Maybe I'd better eat something, to soak up the wine that I just drank so fast. It might help me survive this evening. Plus, I'm hungry.

I'm looking at the menu, trying unsuccessfully to put out the fire that's burning in my cheeks, when Max speaks up again.

"You look lovely tonight," he says. "Is that a new necklace?"

My hand flies to the necklace around my neck. I hold onto the little pouch as Max continues talking. "That looks like a *satchel*, if I'm not mistaken. Let me guess -- the Power Spell?"

"How do you know so much about --" I lower my voice, and look around us to make sure no one is listening. No one is. "--*Witchcraft*," I whisper. "Aren't you a vampire?"

"Penny, one of the great secrets of longevity is curiosity. A healthy dose of curiosity will keep the brain tissue from deteriorating. In fact, curiosity can cause *new* brain cells to grow, and new neurological synapses to form."

"And you're curious about witchcraft?" I ask.

"I'm curious about magic of all sorts," Max says, with a grin. "And yes, I do find witches fascinating. Intriguing. Alluring…"

He's giving me this look, where his dark pupils seem to fuse with mine. I can't tear my eyes away. I feel like he's looking all the way into the depths of me -- wherever that may be. It's making me feel all tingly inside.

Janine approaches, and deliver's Max's glass of Merlot. When he accepts it, he has to look away from me. With relief, I look down at the menu still in my hands.

Whew. This guy is intense.

"Are you thinking about some food?" Janine says, pausing on the other side of the counter, in front of me.

"Oh, uh -- yeah," I say.

"I wouldn't call that 'food', exactly," Max interjects. "Food is defined as a nutritious substance that animals and plants eat, in order to grow and thrive. *That*," he points to the menu, "Isn't nutritious, and certainly isn't going to help you grow -- at least not in the way you want to."

I let the menu fall to the table, and sigh.

Janine's still waiting for my answer.

"You'd be better off peeling the sole of your shoes and eating that, than eating those fries," Max promises.

The thought of eating the bottom of my shoe makes my stomach turn. Maybe I'm not so hungry, after all.

"I'll pass," I say to Janine.

Janine collects the menu and walks away, leaving Max and I alone, again. Without anything else to distract me, I reach for my wine glass. I know that Max is still waiting to know more about my necklace. I don't have to tell him, but I find that I *want* to. Max might actually have some helpful information for me.

"Yeah, it's the Power Spell," I say, keeping my voice low. I'm leaning into him a bit, and he's leaning into me. Our closeness makes me feel woozy, but I don't want anyone to overhear our conversation, and this is the only way to do that.

"I'm not sure if I really believe in it," I whisper. "I've been wearing this thing around since yesterday evening, and nothing has happened. Well, nothing *good* has happened. Nothing that makes me feel more powerful."

Max grins at me. "You are so adorable. You know that, right? Your mind is so linear… it's so precious to listen to you talk."

"I'm glad you get a kick out of this," I say sarcastically. "At least someone does."

"You will too, when you're a seasoned, wise witch looking back on it all." He smiles knowingly.

For a minute I actually feel better. The thought of being a wise *anything* is welcomed, given how clueless I feel at this moment. Then, I feel my frustration and annoyance return.

"What are you talking about… how is my mind linear?" I ask.

"Your mind is conditioned to think in a linear manner," Max says. "It's a pattern all humans are burdened with. In fact, it's one of the four things that make you human. But once you graduate from being human, and you become a magical being, you begin to think differently."

"How?" I ask.

"In spirals," Max says. "Crazy eights. Spheres. Exponential curves. You can think anyway you want to think -- just not linearly. Oh, dear Merlin, no. Linear thinking is dreadfully limiting. It locks you into a past, present, future paradigm, but that's an illusion. Time isn't linear."

I lift my glass to my lips -- a motion I've done several times over the past few minutes, now that I think about it. I'm drinking this glass of wine way too fast, but I can't seem to help it.

"What does that have to do with the Power Spell?" I ask.

Max sips his wine as well. He surveys me as he swallows. I can feel his eyes taking me in.

When he speaks again, his voice is tender. "You're so naive, Penny... so inexperienced. It's very charming. Well, don't you see? You thought that once you put on the necklace, and once the spell began working, you would feel more powerful."

"That's what the book promises!" I say. "I'm counting on it! I *need* to feel more powerful, Max. This thing better kick in soon."

He laughs at my frustration. "It doesn't work like that. First, you might feel *less* powerful. Then, you'll feel your life changing -- pulled in a new direction."

Ug. This does not sound fun. It sounds like a lot of work, actually.

Max continues. "Eventually, you'll circle around to a place with more power... more power than you ever dreamed of, Penny."

My ears perk up. Now *that*, I can handle.

"Really?" I ask.

"Oh, yes," he says, his dark eyes sparkling. "I've seen the transformation happen before. It's always early on in a witch's journey, and it's always beautiful to behold. It's almost like witnessing a birth."

Witnessing a birth doesn't sound beautiful to me. It sounds bloody and painful.

"What if I never figure out what the missing ingredient is?" I ask him.

"Oh, you will. All the witches I've ever known, figured out theirs. Usually within a few days… sometimes up to a week. It all depends on the witch. Don't worry. It will come to you."

"I hope so," I say.

"Tell me, have you been having any dreams lately? Perhaps… vivid dreams?"

"Nope," I say. Then, recalling the dream of clouds I woke up from recently, I correct myself. "Actually, there was one, the other day. I was dreaming that I was above the clouds. I could see them below me."

"Mmm hmm," he says knowingly.

"What does that mean?" I ask.

"You'll see," he says.

"But I want to know now!" I say. My voice rises with frustration. I lower it again. "Max, could you please just be straight with me? This is all really confusing and I could use your help."

"Patience, Penny," he says. "Remember the three Ps?"

"Patience, Persistence, and Playfulness," I recite grudgingly. "The three pillars of witchcraft."

"Good girl," Max says.

I'm thinking back on something he said earlier. Maybe if he won't give me any more clues about the Power

Spell, he'll at least share information about the difference between humans and magical creatures.

"You said that there were four things that define humans," I say. "Linear thinking is one of them. What are the others?" I ask.

"Penny, I'd love to tell you. Really I would. But you're not ready to know. Believe me."

"I *want* to be ready," I say. "This is taking so long. We've been working with the book for months, but it feels like we're getting nowhere. I could *really* use an advantage, right about now."

My shoulders slump, and I look down at the base of my wine glass while I twirl it in my hands.

"Don't tell me..." he says. "Let me guess. Boyfriend trouble?"

I keep staring at the glass I'm fidgeting with as I speak. "This morning, Chris said he had a present for me. He had this little box in his hand, and for a second I thought it was a ring."

Why am I talking to Max, of all people, about this?

I should be talking to Marley, or Cora, or Annie... or *anyone* but Max. Yet here I am, blabbing away. I can't seem to help it.

"An *engagement* ring?" Max asks.

I nod. "The thing is, I always thought that was what I wanted. You know, when I was a teenager, I'd dream about marrying Christopher Wagner. But this morning, when I saw that box, I had this feeling... I'm not sure what it was... but it *wasn't* excitement. I didn't feel that 'yes' that I thought I would."

"It's because you're changing," Max says, carefully. "You and Chris are very different. And the more you learn to harness your magical abilities, the more your sense of being different is going to grow."

"But what if I don't want it to?" I ask.

"Unfortunately -- or fortunately, depending on how you look at it -- you don't really have a choice," says Max. "Magic affects *you*. You're transforming, from the inside out. Humans and magical beings don't make good couples."

"Why not?" I ask.

"Because," says Max. "Humans should be with other humans. And magical beings, we need to be with other magical beings." With this, he gives me a wink.

I flush and meet his eyes. My eyelashes flutter. Oh, good lord.

I need to get out of the OP. The combination of sitting next to Max and drinking wine on an empty stomach is going to my head.

"I need to go," I say abruptly, breaking eye contact and reaching for my bag.

"Good talking with you," Max says. "It's always such a *pleasure*, Penny."

I stand, and walk all the way to the other end of the bar, where Janine is scrubbing glasses.

Janine spots me and flips through her little notebook to my tab. "Are you out of here, hon?" she asks, ripping the bar tab out of her book and placing it before me.

"Yes," I say. After placing a twenty down on top of the tab, I give my face a little fan with one hand. "It's hot in here. Isn't it hot in here? I feel like I need some fresh air."

She shrugs. "I'm cold," she says, while reaching into her apron for change. She places a ten and a few singles on the countertop. I take the ten and leave the singles.

"It might have had something to do with the company you were keeping," she says, glancing down the bar.

I follow her gaze. Max is now chatting with a woman on the other side of him. His profile is visible, and I have to admit to myself that it's handsome. Janine and I stare for a minute, and then Janine whispers, "Damn, he is good looking, isn't he?"

"I don't have any opinion on that," I say.

She laughs. "Right. You're with Captain Chris Wagner. I hear you guys were fooling around with a little bondage scenario up at Mill Creek today." She gives me a wink.

Has *everyone* in this town heard about that? I quickly change the subject, ignoring her comment. "Hey, am I wrong, or is Glenn usually in here every night? I wanted to ask him something."

"Yeah," Janine says. She glances up at the wall clock. "He usually shows up around nine."

I follow her gaze. It's ten of nine.

"So late?" I ask. "I thought I've seen him in here before then."

"Well, he used to come in earlier. But now that he's head chef over at The Place, he says he has more work to take care of before he can leave the kitchen and call it a night."

"Oh," I say. "Right."

"You could just hang out for another few minutes," Janine says. "I'm sure your friend over there wouldn't mind talking with you some more." She tilts her chin in Max's direction.

That's just the problem.

I don't think I can *handle* another ten minutes of sitting next to Max Shire.

"I think I'll head home," I say. "I'll talk to Glenn another night."

"Okay, sweetie," Janine says. She holds up the bills. "Thanks for this. Get home safe, okay?"

"I will," I promise.

I make my way out onto the sidewalk without looking over towards Max once more. I'm afraid that if I look in his direction, he'll catch me staring. He might even lock his gaze with mine, and then I'll feel that crazy, tingly, zappy testosterone-estrogen thing again.

I've had enough of *that* for one night.

I'm a woman in a relationship. A nice, casual, slow-paced relationship. And so what if Max says humans and magical beings can't have good relationships. Max doesn't know what Chris is capable of.

Max doesn't know what *I'm* capable of.

Chris and I have survived so much, already. What's a few more bumps in the road?

It's nothing we can't handle.

At least, that's what I'm hoping.

I take a deep breath of the cool, night air and then unlock my bike. It's dark out now, so I begin walking it down the sidewalk, instead of riding in the street. As I walk, pushing my bike along, I start to imagine ways that I might introduce my magical capabilities to Chris.

'Hey, honey,' I could say, one morning after waking up in his apartment. I'll be standing in the kitchen, wearing one of his oversized tee shirts, and nothing else. I'll be stirring pancake batter. I'll look over at him. He'll be by the coffee machine, holding a mug in one hand and the coffee pot in the other.

'Could you pass me the measuring cup?' I'll ask.

Since his hands are tied up, he'll say something like 'hang on a minute.'

I'll smile. 'Never mind,' I'll say. 'I'll just get it myself.'

I'll lift a little wand off the countertop, and wiggle it in the direction of the cupboards. The measuring cup will start floating towards me.

Chris will smile, his eyes wide with amazement.

'Sugar pie,' he'll say. He's never called me sugar pie, but this is my daydream, and I've always wanted him to call me sugar pie. *'How in the world did you do that?'*

'Oh, I didn't tell you?' I'll say, in answer. 'I've been learning how to be a witch. I can do lots of things.'
'That's amazing, sugar pie.'
He'll finish topping off the steaming cup of coffee. He'll walk over to me, and set it on the table in front of me. Then, before I've even had a chance to use the measuring cups that I so masterfully beckoned to me, he'll sweep me off my feet, and twirl me around the kitchen, while kissing me. In between kisses, he'll say --

"Hey, watch it!" someone says.

I pull myself from my daydream and see that I've almost walked right into Glenn. He's sidestepping me as I barrel forward, head down.

"Oh, sorry!" I say. "I was lost in thought."

Ridiculous, fanciful, unrealistic thought, I realize. There is no *way* that Chris would react to learning about my abilities with a smile and a kiss.

No way.

That's not his style.

I have no idea what he would do, but not that.

Glenn is starting to walk past me.

I turn. I'd rather think about what was going on in The Place's kitchen on the day Joe Gallant died, than think about my boyfriend's potential reaction to the big secret I've been keeping. So, I call out. "Glenn, hang on a sec!"

I steer my bike in a U-turn, and soon I'm walking alongside Glenn.

He's a few years older than me, about Chris's age. He has a babyish face, due to the padding of fat that he wears around his cheeks and chin. His dark, spiky, straight black hair always sticks up in the back, as if he just got out of bed, and tonight is no exception. He's wearing a stained tee shirt and checkered chef pants, and there's a thick silver chain around his neck.

"What?" he asks, as I fall into step with him. His tone isn't nervous or demanding, nor does he display the 'oh-this-girl-must-be-hitting-on-me' attitude that Ralph did, earlier today. Instead, he simply sounds tired.

"Long shift?" I ask. "I heard you're getting out later than you're used to, now that you are the head chef. You must be exhausted."

"Eh," he replies, noncommittally.

"Heading to the OP?" I ask.

"Yeah," he says.

"Cool, cool." We walk in step for a few more strides. "Hey, uh... I have a question for you," I say. "Were you working on the day that Joe Gallant was found?"

He turns his head, and looks at me, but I keep looking straight ahead.

"What, are you with the newspaper or something?" he asks.

I can see the OP up ahead. When we reach the door, I'm going to lose him. There's no way I'm going back inside that bar.

"No," I say. "I'm..." Come on, come on, I think to myself. Think of something! Nothing comes.

"Oh, that's right. You're a detective, aren't you?" Glenn says.

"Exactly," I say.

As if that explains everything, he looks away from me, and starts talking. "Yeah, I was there. When I got into work, Ralph told me that Joe never turned up for his shift. Ralph said that he called Joe but Joe didn't answer."

"Would that be normal?" I ask. "For Ralph to call Joe, I mean."

"Sure," says Glenn. "Ralph was always doing stuff that Cliff couldn't get to. Ralph was Cliff's right hand guy. If one of us didn't show up for work, it would be normal for Ralph to give us a call to see what the holdup was about."

"Okay," I say. "Then what?"

"Ralph told me to get started on the prep work. We had a bunch of salads to make, and those take a lot of time; tuna, potato, pasta… pretty intensive, you know. I put on some tunes and got to chopping. When Cliff came in, he found Joe in the walk in."

"So, you're saying Ralph *told* you Joe wasn't in for the day? And Ralph says he called Joe, but Joe didn't answer?" I ask, to make sure I heard him right.

"Yeah," Glenn says. We reach the door, and he places his hand on the handle.

"Are you sure?" I ask.

"Yeah, I'm sure," Glenn says. "If no one had told me that Joe was out for the day, I would have called him myself. My guess is that Joe was already stuck in the deep freezer when Ralph came in, or something. Ralph must not have known."

Hunh, I think, as I watch Glenn pull the door open.

"Coming in?" he asks, holding the door open for me.

Beyond him, I can see the back of Max's head.

"No!" I say, a bit too loud. "Glenn -- before you go in, I just have one more question," I say.

Glenn looks longingly into the bar. The man is thirsty for his post-shift beer, I can see. "Is Ralph a good boss?" I ask.

Glenn shrugs. "He's alright," he says. "He takes off on the weekends sometimes, which can be a pain because those are our busiest days -- Saturdays and Sundays. And he doesn't help out as much around the kitchen as Cliff did, but, *eh*," he shrugs. "As far as bosses go, things could be worse."

"Where does he go?" I ask. "When he takes off."

"Up to his cabin on Rainbow lake," Glenn answers. "To fish. He's always inviting people up there with him. I think he's pretty proud of the place."

"I didn't know there were cabins on Rainbow lake," I say, thinking of the alpine lake about a mile up a trail to the north of town. "There isn't even a road that goes up there."

As I'm trying to remember what I can about the lake, Rebecca, our town librarian squeezes past Glenn to get to the sidewalk. I make room for her and then return to my place.

"Yeah, you have to hike up, and there's only one cabin," Glenn says. "It's in Ralph's family -- he inherited it. It was put up before the lake was turned into a water reserve. I've fished up there -- lots of rainbow trout."

I change topics before Glenn can start talking fishing, which I know from experience with other mountain men can turn into quite the tangent. I want to squeeze all the info out of Glenn that I can, while I've got him. I don't want to chit chat about where the good fishing is. "Do you think Mayor Haywater was going to choose Joe over Ralph, before the 'accident' with the freezer occurred?" I ask.

Glenn looks over his shoulder into the bar again, and waves as he spots a friend. He seems distracted when he looks back to me. I'm losing him!

"I thought you said *one* more question?" Glenn asks me.

"Please, Glenn," I beg. "This is important."

Glenn sighs. "Okay -- do I think Mayor Haywater was going to choose Joe or Ralph. You know, I was pretty sure Cliff was going to go with Joe. All of us were, actually. I think the entire staff is pretty surprised to be reporting to Ralph now, but we're making it work. Now, I really need a beer."

I open my mouth to protest, but before I can speak the OP door is closing in my face.

My mind begins turning over what I just learned.

Ralph knew that Joe didn't turn up for work? Ralph called Joe, to see where he was?

This is *not* what Ralph reported, earlier today. Ralph was adamant that he had gone straight to the office, and had no idea that Joe was missing. Ralph said that he had worked right up until the paramedics arrived.

Ralph's and Glenn's stories don't match. One of them has to be lying, I think, as I steer my bike in another U-turn.

But who?

Chapter Ten

The next morning, I'm heading down the walkway towards the sidewalk in front of my apartment unit when I catch sight of a head of blue hair, bobbing up and down, behind a very full cardboard box.

I *recognize* that blue hair.

Pausing, I wait for the woman to slow down. As she passes by me, I look over. Yep. It's Azure Spincraft, leader of the Air Coven of witches.

Azure and I met in July, when I was first learning about my witchy abilities. Back then, she wanted to steal ASBW from me, and take over the portal into Hillcrest. She thought it was dangerous to have a portal into the Earth Realm guarded by inexperienced witches.

"Azure?" I say, as our eyes meet.

She sets the box down with a thud.

Azure is slender and pretty, and about my age. Her long blue hair is pulled up in a bun, held in place with Chinese chopsticks. She's wearing purple lipstick.

"Penny! Fancy running into you here," she says with a mischievous glint in her pale blue eyes.

"I live right upstairs," I say. "You *know* that. You tried to break into my apartment to steal my book, remember?"

"Ha! *Your* book. As if a book that has been around for millennia could really belong to *you*."

"It's in my possession," I argue. "Claudine Terra gave it to me." I fold my arms across my chest. "The book says that I'm destined to become a witch. It's my *destiny*, Azure. Don't act like it's a mistake."

"Are you *sure* it's your destiny to be a witch?" she asks. "Wouldn't you be better at it, if it was really your destiny?"

I don't have a response to this, so I point to her box again. "What are you doing here, with that box?" I ask.

"Oh, this," she says. "This is just a portion of my herbs and tinctures collection. About a fifth of it, actually."

I eye the box. It's about three feet wide, and three feet tall. "That's a lot of herbs," I say. And then, "Why are you carrying all that around here?" I ask.

"I'm moving in," Azure says, motioning to the door we've stopped in front of. It's unit B.

Crap.

"Excuse me?" I say.

"I think you heard me," Azure says. She places a hand on the hip of her skinny jeans and turns her purple lips down into a pout. "What's wrong, you don't want to have me as a neighbor?"

"You can't be moving in here," I say. "You're an air witch. Don't you live in another realm?"

"I'm not moving in full time," Azure says. "Goddess, no. This place is… ug," she makes a face as she looks around. "So earthy. Look at this, dirt, rocks, grass, wood, rusty steel."

She gives the corrugated siding of the building a rap with her knuckles. "I feel about a hundred pounds heavier the minute I enter through the portal."

"I believe that's rusty *tin*," I say. I don't like the way she's talking about my home. What's wrong with dirt, rocks, and grass? True, I've never been anywhere else, but the Earth Realm doesn't seem so bad to me.

"Steel… tin, whatever," Azure says. "It's all metal to me. Heavy metal. Where I'm from, there is nothing this dense. Honestly, I don't know how you live with it full time. I'm going to have to take a lightness-tincture every few hours just to sustain myself."

"If you think it's so horrible here, why are you moving in part time?" I ask.

"Someone has to keep an eye on this portal," she says. "As it is now, anyone can enter through it. I don't love the Earth Realm, but I also don't want it to be destroyed. If a being from one of the dark realms chooses to come in through that portal, they could wreak havoc... not just in Hillcrest, but anywhere on Earth that they wanted to."

"My coven and I can defend Hillcrest," I say. "And... the Earth. We're not helpless, you know."

She raises an eyebrow. "Really? I think that a goblin from the Fire Realm could waltz in here and do whatever he wanted, and you wouldn't know where to *begin* in stopping him. It would be easy for him... too easy. Like stealing Payday candy bars from the Hillcrest Market."

Wait just one minute. That reference is far too specific.

I narrow my eyes. "Have you been watching me?" I ask.

She waves a hand. "Oh, don't act so offended. It's a simple spy-glass spell. You'll be doing it all the time once you get the hang of it."

"That's an invasion of my privacy!" I say.

Just how much has she been spying on me? Clearly, she knows what I've been up to at work. What about at home?

Has she been watching me while I'm in the apartment?

In my bedroom?

In the -- oh, no -- the *bathroom*? I spend five minutes a day doing mirror work, like Jumper Strongheart instructs in his book 'A More Confident You'. As per the instructions he offers, I stare into the mirror and repeat: 'I am confident! I am strong! I am unstoppable!'

And yes, sometimes it turns into chanting, or perhaps even a song or two -- complete with hairbrush microphone.

"Nice singing, by the way," Azure says, confirming my worst fears. She *has* been spying on me during my special bathroom time!

"That is so not cool!" I say.

"There's no such thing as privacy for witches, Penny," Azure says. "Not that you're a real witch or anything, but since you're *pathetically* trying to be one, you'd better know that. It's not one of the three P's, is it?"

I have to think for a minute. Patience. Persistence. Playfulness.

"No..." I shake my head.

She continues. "That's because it goes out the window when you enter into the profession. Telepathy is pretty much mind reading, and every witch has a familiar, which is basically an extension of self. Then, there's the bonding that happens between a coven... you know, shared energy and all of that."

She waves a hand nonchalantly. "Only humans believe in privacy, and it's one of the four things that keeps them ridiculously limited."

"Four things?" I repeat. "I think Max was just telling me about that. What are the others?"

"You are *so* not ready to know that," Azure says.

Now it's my turn to pout. "Why does everyone keep telling me that?" I ask. "I *am* ready! I wouldn't be putting myself through all of this if I wasn't ready. This isn't exactly easy, you know, or fun."

I'm thinking of Chris, now. It definitely isn't fun feeling different than him. My pout sinks into a full-on frown.

"Oh, cheer up," Azure says. "Being a witch is the best calling out there. You'll know that if you ever actually become one. Which, I doubt you will."

Then she reaches into her sleeve and pulls out a small twig. She waves it at Unit B's door and says, "Reserare!"

The door flies open.

"Door handles are so unhygienic," she mutters, as she stoops to pick up the box. "And who has the patience for house keys?"

"Not me," I say.

"Well, nice chatting with you. I've got some unpacking to do. I can feel my lightness-tincture wearing off."

With that, she disappears into the apartment.

Great.

What a way to start my day! I'm filled with so much doubt that I almost want to run upstairs and lock myself in the bathroom for a round of 'I am confident, I am strong!' work. Maybe I'll add in, 'It is my destiny to be a witch!'

It's going to take a while for *that* one to feel true.

Jumper says that if you keep on repeating something, eventually your mind starts to accept it. He calls it an affirmation.

I really do think that saying 'I am confident' while staring into the mirror has helped me. I used to feel like an absolute liar when I said it, and now I only feel like I'm stretching the truth.

If I affirmed that it was my destiny to be a witch over and over, would it eventually be true?

Will the word 'destiny' ever stop feeling too big and grand, for little old me?

Since I'm already off to a late start, I decide against retreating to my bathroom for mirror work. Instead, I repeat the mantra in my head as I ride to my supply closet -- I mean office!

At my desk, I stare down at my list of suspects. And stare. And stare. And stare.

A whole hour goes by this way.

Joe Gallant: Murder Suspects

5. *Ralph*
6. *Glenn*
7. *Cliff*
8. *Melanie*

While I look at the names, I'm going over all the information that I've gathered so far.

The whole mess reminds me a lot of the tangled yarn that's stuffed in my desk drawer, out of sight. I wish I could put this jumbled mess of clues out of mind, too, but I can't.

For one thing, I *really* owe Cliff an update on the case. For another, I'm more sure than ever before that Joe Gallant was murdered. Why else would I have uncovered so many lies?

Ralph and Glenn told me different stories, so one of them is hiding something. On top of that, Melanie was acting *very* suspicious.

There has to be something more going on.

I'm onto something big -- and I may be the only one. According to Chris, the police have written off Joe's death as an accident.

But if he was murdered, that means that there is a killer in Hillcrest.

I may not yet be a witch, yet, but I *am* a certified private investigator. I can figure this out. It's my job.

I just have to think.

And knit.

I think better, when my hands are busy.

I take out my scarf project, and begin working furiously.

My scarf, which is already too long, starts to grow. The crooked, bumpy monstrosity is pooling on the floor by the time its two o'clock, and my phone rings.

I look at the screen.

Shoot.

It's Cliff Haywater!

I'm not ready to talk to him. I'm aware that I have to tell him about the divorce papers, but I don't know how! Panicking, I hit the button on the side of my phone that will forward him to voicemail.

The ringing stops.

Phew! That was a close one.

I pick up my needles, and just as I begin to knit, the ringing starts up again.

It's Cliff, a second time!

No!

I forward it to voicemail, feeling extra guilty as I do so.

When he calls a third time, I cringe. Crap. I really can't avoid this call, can I?

I pick up.

"Hello?" I say, tentatively.

"Penny! Good, I caught you. This is Cliff Haywater."

As if I didn't know. "Hi Cliff. I've been meaning to call you, actually," I say.

"Oh, you have? Good! Do you know where she is?" he asks.

"Who?" I ask.

"What do you mean, *who*? My wife!" He sounds annoyed. "You've been keeping an eye on her, haven't you?"

"Keeping an eye on her? No, Mayor Haywater. I haven't been watching your wife. I don't do surveillance like that. You can't find her?"

"She said she'd be home from her nail appointment by lunch time. She was going to make quiche, and we were going to have lunch together at noon. It was important. But now it's two in the afternoon!"

"It is?" Whew! Time flies when you're thinking and knitting. "I'm sure she's fine," I say. "Why was lunch so important?"

He doesn't answer me. "So, you have no idea where she is?" he asks.

"None," I say.

"But you did call that Express Travel company, about the ticket?" he asks.

I bite my lip. "No," I say, after a moment.

"Oh. You talked to Gale, though? I'm sure she had some insight into all of this."

"Um… I haven't gotten to that either, quite yet," I say.

He's quiet for a moment, so I interject. "Why was lunch so important, Cliff?" I ask again.

This time he answers. "I was going to give her a gift," he says. "I got us two plane tickets to Hawaii. Oahu, actually. I just bought them this morning, they were on sale. I was going to surprise her with them."

"Oh." Maybe I should have told him about the divorce papers yesterday after all. "Are those tickets refundable, by any chance?" I ask

"Refundable? No! It's for a trip next week. Melanie is always saying how I work too much, and I thought surprising her with a vacation would be just the thing to cheer her up. I have a hotel booked, too. It was all a lot to arrange in such a short notice. She's going to have to clear her schedule, which is why I wanted to tell her today."

Since Melanie doesn't work, I'm sure clearing her schedule is going to be the least of her concerns. Canceling a few hair and nail appointments surely won't be that difficult to do. As I think about Melanie's schedule, the memory of her planner pops into my mind. I really have to talk to Bess about the Melanie's visit to the Antique Haven on the day that Joe died.

Cliff continues. "But now, I don't know where she is. I called the nail salon and they said she left four hours ago!"

"Maybe she went for a walk in the park," I say. "Or to the market…"

"It's not like Melanie," Cliff says. "I know my wife. When she says she'll be somewhere, she's there. She told me she would be home at eleven fifteen. She even asked me to defrost the quiche, so that it would be ready for her to bake. Now it's sitting on the counter-top. It was sweating out little drops of water, and now it's resting in a wet pool. It's getting warm and I don't know what to do with it."

"Put it in the refrigerator," I suggest. "I'm sure she'll be home soon, and she can bake it then."

I want to hang up, but Cliff isn't going to let me get away that easily.

"If you haven't been watching my wife, and you haven't called Express Travel, and you haven't talked to Gale, what exactly *have* you been doing?" he asks.

I bounce a little bit on my Swiss ball, nervously.

"Uh… er… I've been… well, I did talk to your wife, sir," I say.

Should I tell him about the divorce papers? Now? I can picture him, standing in his kitchen next to the sad, defrosted, sweaty quiche. It almost breaks my heart.

"Is that all? You *talked* to her? Anyone could do that. I didn't pay you three hundred dollars just to talk to her," Cliff says, cutting through the silence. "I thought you were a detective. I mean, I had my doubts when I visited your office, but I thought you could be helpful."

I know I should defend myself. But the words simply don't come.

"You know what?" Cliff says. "This isn't working out, is it? It was a mistake to hire you, I'm afraid. I'd like my money back."

"Sir…" I say quietly. My hand flies to the satchel hanging around my neck.

You know how we had to write down our fears, and then burn the paper to make ash?

Well, *this* is my worst fear.

I wrote down the word 'Failure' on that little slip of paper.

Now, Cliff is saying that I failed him.

I'm speechless.

I already pushed the money that he gave me under Sherry's door. I couldn't get it back, even if I wanted to. Plus, even if I did manage to get it back from Sherry, I would still owe her rent.

My mind has already started to spiral downwards, and I'm missing what Cliff is saying now as I keep traveling down a path of negative thinking.

If I can't pay rent, I'll have to move out of my office. Without an office, how will I get new clients? Maybe Chris was right to not take my PI business seriously. Maybe my career is a joke.

"-- tomorrow at noon," Cliff says.

Then, there's silence.

He's waiting for my response.

I clear my throat. Could this conversation get any worse? "Sorry," I say. "I kind of zoned out there for a minute. What did you just say?"

"I *said*, I'll be stopping by your office for my refund tomorrow at noon," Cliff repeats. Yep. He is definitely annoyed.

"Okay," I mumble. "Got it."

"Goodbye, Penny." Without another word, Cliff hangs up.

I'm left staring down at my phone.

What am I going to do now?

I guess I have no other option.

I need to have money, to repay Cliff. I'm going to have to do something as far from respectable PI work as I can imagine.

I've always had confidence issues -- since I was a little kid, growing up poor with a single mom. I never really felt good enough. My thick glasses, frizzy hair, lack of coordination and mouth full of braces didn't help.

Being prideful has never been an issue for me.

However, if I *did* have any pride to start out with, I'm sure I'd be swallowing it now, as I dial the lawyer that Cora works for, Hiroku Itsu.

"Hello?" I say, when Hiroku answers. "This is Penny… Penny Banks. Cora gave me your number. I'd like to talk to you about becoming a…." I pause, in disbelief. Has my life really come to this?

Yes.

Yes, it has.

I take a deep breath. "I'd like to talk to you about becoming a nanny for your Chihuahua."

Chapter Eleven

I plan to meet Hiroku at her offices at four. Apparently, her Chihuahua, Blueberry Muffin, will be there as well, so that we can 'get to know each other'.

The only thing that makes this situation any better is that Hiroku agreed to give me a three-hundred-dollar advance payment.

I'll have money to give to Cliff, tomorrow.

Since I have two hours 'til I have to report for my new nanny duties, and learning the Chihuahua's name stirred my appetite, I head off to the Death Cafe to see if Annie has been doing any baking.

When I enter the cafe, the smell of freshly baked pie greets me. Finally, something is going right!

I make my way to the counter, and Annie smiles when she sees me.

"Penny! I was hoping you would stop by. How is the case coming along?"

"I was fired," I say.

"Fired! By Mayor Haywater?"

I nod.

She shakes her head. "What is that man thinking? First he bans awnings because the sidewalks are 'too narrow' and now he fires the best PI in town?"

"The *only* PI in town," I say.

"Oh, you poor thing. Well, have some pie. On the house."

Who can say no to that? I graciously accept the fat wedge of peach pie that Annie serves up to me, and then start eating it while I'm still standing at the counter. There're only a few other patrons in the cafe, and no one waiting to order or pay, so I know Annie doesn't mind.

"What happened?" Annie asks, as I begin wolfing down pie.

"Cliff called… he wanted to know what I've been doing to figure out why his wife bought the one-way ticket. I couldn't tell him about the progress I made -- you know, the divorce papers -- without dragging Cora into it."

"I suppose not," Annie says.

"Plus," I add, "I don't *want* to tell him about the divorce. He should hear that from his wife, not me."

"But what about Joe Gallant?" Annie asks.

She reaches below the counter for something, and then places it on the countertop next to my plate of pie. I see that it's Joe's obituary.

"Here," she says, pushing the paper towards me. "I cut that out of the Crier weeks ago. I was going to put it up on the wall in the bathroom, but then I thought you should have a look at it first."

"Thanks," I say. While most of the Death Cafe is decorated cheerfully, the bathroom decor stays true to the death theme. It is wallpapered in obituaries. "I'll bring it back to you once I read it," I promise.

Annie nods. "Do you still think he was murdered?"

Good question. I chew and swallow my pie. "I do," I say. "I'm not really sure what to do about that."

"Keep trying to figure out who killed him!" Annie says.

"You think I should?" I ask.

"What kind of a question is that?" Annie asks. She reaches out and pats my arm. "Of *course,* you should." A timer starts beeping, and Annie grins. "That's my macaroons!" she says, and hustles off.

While she's gone, I scan over the obituary.

It's pretty short. It says that Joe Gallant grew up in Hillcrest, the youngest of two brothers. His older brother, Paul Gallant, was a plow truck driver for the town. Paul died three years back, of a heart attack. Joe had no children, and is survived by his niece, Paul's only daughter, Molly Gallant.

I know Molly. She works at the Art Coop, over by the library.

Annie returns, with a tray bursting with steaming, fragrant macaroons.

I look up from the obituary. "This is helpful," I tell my friend. "I forgot that Joe had a niece."

"Good, I thought it might be. Will you talk to Molly?"

"I'd love to," I say. "Eventually. But I'm going to have to put this investigation on hold while I figure out the ins and outs of this new gig I just took on. I'm going to be a --" I stop short, unable to say the words aloud.

"A what?" Annie asks, raising her brow.

"A… well, a nanny for a very high maintenance Chihuahua," I say.

Annie laughs. Then, meeting my stony gaze, she stops abruptly. "Oh, dear!" she says. "You're serious?"

I nod. "It's just a couple of afternoons a week, and I'll make twenty dollars an hour. I'm going to find out more about it soon."

"Here," she says, reaching for a pair of tongs. "Have a macaroon. It will cheer you up."

I hold up a hand. I've polished off the slice of pie and I'm feeling full. "No," I say. "I can't accept your pity pastries." I say.

"Just one little macaroon?" Annie says. She already has it in the tongs, and she's holding it out towards me, waving it back and forth in front of my nose. It smells so good!

"Oh, okay," I say. How could I say no?

As I break it in two to let some of the steam escape, I continue lamenting my position.

"It's my own fault I was fired," I say. "I should have just done what Cliff told me. He wanted me to call the Express Travel people and talk to Melanie's sister Gale. I didn't do those things."

My shoulders slump. "It's my fault for getting fired from the case, and it's my fault that I have to resort to Chihuahua nannying."

"Penny, Cliff Haywater is not a detective -- *you're* the detective. He can't tell you how to solve a case. You have a natural ability with this kind of thing. You were following your instincts! Your instincts as an investigator, and..." she lowers her voice. "Your instincts as a witch."

"Thanks," I say, biting into the now cooler macaroon. It's fluffy and sweet.

Annie speaks as I chew. "If I were you, I'd --"

I don't' get to hear what Annie would do, because at that moment a woman enters the cafe, talking loudly. "Is that *peach pie* I smell?" she gushes.

She rushes up to the counter, and I move to the side to get out of her way.

"Oh, Annie, dear, I just *knew* I smelled it from outside! You know how I love your pie. Look, Savannah! Annie made her peach pie!"

The woman turns to the door, and calls out loudly to a toddler who has just wobbled in.

At first, I try to wait for the woman to order and then go away, so that I can keep talking to my friend. I polish off my macaroon and hover around the counter. But the woman has a myriad of questions for Annie, and while they're talking, two more customers gather round the counter, drawn in by the smell of freshly baked pie and macaroons.

I can see that Annie will be tied up for longer than I have the patience to wait.

"I'll talk to you later," I tell Annie, as I pick up my crumb-riddled plate and the Crier clipping.

"Good luck, Penny," Annie says over her shoulder as she pours a cup of coffee from a carafe behind the counter. "Don't give up!" She gives me a wink, and then returns to pouring coffee.

On my way out the door, I deposit the plate into a dustbin, and I fold the obituary in half and slide it into the back pocket of my messenger bag. I can feel the cuffs in the pocket too, exactly where I left them. I'll have to pick out a key ring soon, like Chris suggested.

Out on the sidewalk, I consider Annie's words.

Just because Cliff *fired* me doesn't mean I have to stop searching for the truth. I *want* to know why Melanie booked that flight, and never took it. I *want* to know who killed Joe.

I glance at my phone. I have an hour before I have to be at Hiroku's office. That's just enough time for a quick visit to Bess' Antique Haven.

When I step into the Antique Haven, I spot Bess at the back, rearranging a row of used cowboy boots up on a high shelf. As I walk over, I eye the boots in her hand. They're burnished red, with little hand painted, turquoise and pink roses on the side. Since I'm here on business, not for shopping, I make myself look away.

"Hi there, Penny," Bess says warmly as I approach. "Just got these in!" She holds out the boots, and wiggles them in my direction. "They're your size, and would look great on you... seeing as you've been wearing so much black lately. You should really accessorize with a bit of color."

I *have* been wearing alot of black lately, and the black high-tops I have on do nothing to spice up my outfit. Those boots would look great with some of my dresses...

No! I am here on business!

Bess is about to say something else, but I hold up a hand to stop her. "No, thanks," I say. "They're really nice, but I'm not here to shop."

She looks disappointed by this, but she puts the boots up on the shelf and starts climbing off her step ladder.

"Oh? Then what can I do for you?" she asks.

"I'm here on *PI* business," I say. I like the way it sounds. I puff up my chest a bit as I continue. "I'm hoping that you can tell me a bit about Melanie Haywater's visit to you, on the fourteenth of last month."

"Penny," Bess says, making her way through the racks of consignment and vintage clothing. "I could barely tell you what I had for breakfast this morning. How am I supposed to tell you what happened last month?"

I follow her. Bess walks behind the shop's counter and takes a seat on a padded stool by the cash register. Her glasses are hanging down on a beaded chain, resting on her ample chest. She lifts them up to her eyes and peers at me. "And why do you want to know about Melanie Haywater, anyways?"

"It's PI business," I say. "Like I said."

"I don't like it," Bess says, shaking her head. Some of her warm tone is gone. "You always seem to be rooting around in other people's business, Penny Banks. How would you like it if I went around snooping into *your* personal matters?"

"Snoop all you want," I say. Then, thinking of my recent conversation with Azure, I add. "Privacy is overrated, anyways."

Bess makes a *tisk tisk* sound with her tongue. She looks down at a pile of receipts and starts idly flipping through them.

I continue. "This is for everyone's safety," I say. "There might be a murderer in our town, and I, for one, am not too happy about that."

Bess snaps her head up, and her fingers stop flipping through the papers. "A murderer?" she repeats.

I nod solemnly. "I'm not positive, Bess, but I've been looking into Joe Gallant's death and it really doesn't seem like an accident to me."

"Oh, my!" Bess places a hand on her bosom. "Well, I had no idea! Here I am going about business as if everything is just fine! All the while there's a killer prowling about. Are the police after him?"

"Or *her*," I say, correcting Bess. I think about Chris's response to my suggestion that Joe was killed. *'Don't go imagining things,'* I can hear him say.

I screw my lips up to the side. "The police? Er… not exactly." I say. "And I don't have any hard evidence. Not enough to get the PD to start up an investigation. So, I'm investigating this myself."

Bess nods. "Alright, then," she says, as if I've passed some sort of test. "And what does Melanie Haywater have to do with all of this? I saw her at the salon when I was getting my hair done the other day." Bess gives her short, died auburn locks a loving pat. "She *really* didn't look good. Pale and tired, if you ask me."

"Melanie was at The Place on the day that Joe was found dead," I say. "I'm looking into everyone that was there that day, not just Melanie. I want to be thorough. In her planner, it said that --"

"How do you know what she has written in her planner?" Bess interrupts to ask me.

I wave a hand. "I just happened to see it, when I was over for coffee…" I say.

"You and Melanie have coffee together?" Bess asks.

"Once in a while," I answer. Once, period, I think to myself. "Anyways, I saw that she came *here* right before she went into The Place that day. It was in the middle of the afternoon. About two thirty. She had an appointment with you. Does that ring any bells?"

"Hmm… let me see…" Bess taps her lips as she thinks. "Middle of the day… that would be right after lunch hour… unless I ate early, which I do sometimes…"

I give her time. Eventually, after much lip-tapping and verbalized musings, Bess comes up blank.

"I'm sorry, Penny," she says. "I'd love to help you, but I see so many people every day, and I just don't think I can recall one specific transaction like that."

Well, at least one of our businesses is booming. I wish *I* was having trouble keeping transactions straight.

Bess goes on. "Now, if you asked me about those painted cowboy boots that I just got in today, I could tell you all the details. Buttercup brought them in. She was waiting outside when I opened up the shop, and she said that --"

I don't mean to be rude, but I can't stand here and listen to a long winded story that doesn't pertain to our case, so I interrupt. "Would you have it in your paperwork?" I ask, pointing to the pile of receipts that Bess has at her fingertips.

"Oh! Goodness. You're right! Penny, you're a clever one. Has anyone ever told you that?"

I adjust my glasses. Yes, people have told me that, but I never tire of hearing it. Fake it 'til you make it actually works! I've been complimented on my intelligence *eleven* times since I started wearing these thick-rimmed glasses! Eleven!

Bess reaches down below the counter, and pulls out a thick maroon binder. It's bursting at the seams with papers. I eye the massive conglomeration of paperwork skeptically. There are little yellow and pink slips of paper poking out here and there. Is Bess going to be able to find anything in this massive binder?

The answer is yes. Bess flips right to a page in the back end of the book.

"Here we are," she says, leaning over the book and peering through her rhinestone-studded glasses. "A receipt that I wrote out to Melanie, on August fourteenth. Looks like she picked up clothes from me. You're right. It was two thirty-nine when she left the shop."

"And she was picking up clothes?" I ask.

"Right. A whole lot of them... by the looks of this receipt. Here I wrote 'Vineyard Vines Tropical Printed sundress'. Oh! That's right. I do remember that dress. A lovely little summer number."

Bess stares into the distance for a moment, as if visualizing the dress. She smiles fondly, and then returns her attention to the receipt. "And here I have "Flamingo Sleeveless Blouse'. Yes, it was a whole order of summer beach clothes. I remember thinking how odd that was, seeing as the Haywaters never go on vacation."

She makes that *tisk tisk* sound again, and then continues. "Her choices didn't make sense, and she was very close-lipped about it. But then again, I was having that sale on summer wear, and I was selling a lot of it. I sold that whole dozen of the Hawaiian shirts that were marked down, just the day before."

"Her choices *do* make sense," I say. "She had a plane ticket booked for Hawaii."

"She did? Well! She didn't tell me that."

"Yeah, well... she didn't tell her *husband*, either," I say, under my breath.

Oops. Bess must have heard me, because she says, "Oh, dear. That's not good, is it?" she asks.

I shake my head. I don't want to gossip about the Haywaters' marriage, but I *do* want to get to the bottom of this case. So I stay quiet, giving Bess the opportunity to go on, as I know she will.

I'm right.

"They haven't seemed very happy, these past few years," Bess says. "I overheard Melanie once, when we were both getting our hair done." Bess gives her cared-for auburn doo another gentle pat. "She was lamenting the good old days, when she was in her twenties and everything felt exciting. She said that the spark was gone..."

"Do you think they might be headed for divorce?" I ask.

Bess nods. "I wouldn't be surprised," she says.

Then, we both fall silent. Neither of us is above a little bit of gossip, but I can sense that we've reached our limit. Bess doesn't want to harp on the sorry state of the Haywaters' marriage, and neither do I.

"Well, thank you for looking that up for me," I say.

"You're welcome," Bess says. She points a finger at me. "And *you* think about those boots," she says. "They're one of a kind, and would really do wonders for your wardrobe. I've got them marked at seventy-five dollars, but I'll sell them to you for fifty."

"Thank you," I say. "Maybe I'll come back for them."

"Do you want me to hold them for you?" she asks. "Because if I don't, they might go before you return. I know someone in this town is going to snap them up." Bess gives her fingers a little snap. "I have an eye for things that will go quickly."

"No, you don't have to hold them," I say. Then, "Bess, one more thing, really quick." I know that I have to get going soon, if I want to get to the law office on time. But something Bess said has been tickling my consciousness.

"You said that someone bought a dozen Hawaiian shirts, the day before. Who was it?"

"Right. I'd almost forgotten about that..." Bess says. "I was so happy to be getting rid of all that summer wear. If I don't sell it, it just sits in the back all winter. Now that I think about it though, I think that bag of shirts is *still* sitting in the back."

Bess has been leafing through her binder, and now she points her finger to the page.

"Here it is -- the receipt!" She scans it quickly. "My, my, my. What a funny coincidence!"

"What?" I ask.

"Well, this customer who bought the shirts. He picked them all out and paid on the thirteenth -- I remember now -- and was going to come back to get them on the fourteenth, so that I'd have time to steam out the wrinkles. I do hate selling things with wrinkles. But he never came back. Now I know why!"

She looks up at me with surprise.

"Why?" I ask.

"Because," she says, her eyes wide. "He died! I sold all of those Hawaiian shirts to Joe Gallant!"

Chapter Twelve

Why did Joe Gallant buy up a dozen Hawaiian shirts? I wonder, as I ride my bike down the hill from main street towards Hiroku's law office.

Was he planning a vacation too?

Was he planning a vacation *with* Melanie, maybe?

My bike picks up speed, and as I coast, I consider the possibility that Melanie and Joe were going to jet off together. She was getting divorce papers drafted, after all. Maybe it was because there was another man in the picture.

Phew. I'm kind of glad that I don't have to report back to Cliff any more. It was going to be bad enough telling him about the divorce, I can't imagine having to tell him that his wife was interested in another man.

I'm whizzing along the street now, and I can hear Chris's voice, playing in my mind again: 'Don't go imagining things'.

I can't help it! I argue back, mentally, of course. See? I can't help but imagine things. Now I'm imagining a conversation with Chris!

I'm an imaginative woman. Some might say that's why I'm well suited to be a private investigator.

Oh, shoot! I just zoomed passed the law office. I hit my bike brakes hard, and they squeal as my bike lurches and skids to a stop. Several pedestrians swivel their heads to look in my direction.

I wave. Nothing to see here!

As I steer my bike in a U-turn, my thoughts change direction too. *Am* I a good private investigator?

I did just get fired from the first real case I've had in months.

Maybe my wild imagination makes me a *poor* private investigator. The fact that Joe bought a dozen Hawaiian shirts around the same time that Melanie did, could really just be a coincidence. Joe may have been browsing the store, and noticed the shirts were on sale. All of us love to find a bargain, right?

I dismount my bike, and search around for somewhere to lock it.

Joe could have simply been a bargain hunter, but that would be so boring, I think, as I begin strapping my bike lock around a tree. It is much more exciting to think that Melanie and Joe were heading off on a scandalous vacation to Hawaii together.

I think the Hawaiian shirts are a clue. But how do they fit in with Joe's death?

I wish I could go straight back to my office and create a mind map of the case.

Mind maps were covered in my PI program. They involve lots of circles and lines and are supposed to help detectives make connections.

A few connections would really be useful, right about now!

Unfortunately, mind mapping in my office is not in my immediate future.

Blueberry Muffin, the high-maintenance Chihuahua, is waiting to meet me.

When I walk into Hiroku Law Office, I see Cora sitting behind her desk. She's typing away busily but spots me out of the corner of her eye.

"Penny!" she says happily, jumping up from her chair. "You never come visit me at work! I feel so honored!"

Wow. I knew that I loved it when my friends visited my office (mostly Marley, when she's in between massage clients), but I never considered the fact that my friends might be waiting for *me* to visit *them*.

Note to self: Visit Cora at work more often.

She looks like I just made her day!

I feel a little bit bad as I say, "I'm actually here to see Hiroku about the nannying gig."

Cora isn't as sensitive as I am. My statement doesn't faze her. In typical Cora fashion, she remains chirpy and upbeat. "Oh, that's great!" she says. "I knew that you'd be interested. I'll go see if she's ready for you."

She turns, blonde ponytail swinging, and I'm left standing in the lobby.

In two minutes, Cora returns, followed by her boss, Hiroku Itsu. The petite Japanese woman is cradling a little Chihuahua, who, I can see, is appropriately named. The little mutt looks almost *exactly* like a blueberry muffin.

Seeing me, the muffin barks. It's a high-pitched, yipping sound that pierces through the air in the office.

"Oh?" Hiroku says, stroking the top of the muffin's head. She looks at me. "Blueberry Muffin says that you're a cat person."

The dog is darn right. I *am* a cat person. I just realized that, when I flinched at the sound of that bark. Cats don't bark. I hadn't realized how much I favored sophisticated, quiet, fluffy, cuddly cats over yippy rambunctious dogs until just now. Apparently, this dog realized the same thing. How did he know that?

Just as I'm about to ask, Hiroku pulls a bow from her pocket, and clips it to the hair on the top of the muffin's head, and I have to revise my thoughts. How did *she* know that?

"Blueberry is very perceptive," Hiroku says. "She also has a powerful sense of smell. I think she can smell cat on you"

I frown. Did this woman just tell me I smell like a cat? Should I take offense to that? *Hm.*

I want to deliver a rebuttal, but I better keep my attitude in check if I want this job.

"Does, she, um... *like* cats?" I ask, meekly. I really need this job, and this is pretty much my interview -- as sad as that is.

Hiroku takes a moment to think over my question.

Cora shoots me a thumbs up, and mouths "good luck!" before sneaking back to her computer.

After a moment of tense silence, Hiroku says, "Blueberry likes *some* cats. Not all cats. She's very particular. And she only likes *certain* people, too."

"Does she like me?" I ask, tentatively.

Blueberry Muffin yips again. Twice.

Hiroku nods. Then she says, "Blue doesn't *love* you because your energy makes her a little bit nervous, but you're our only option right now. No offense, I'm just letting you know how she feels. I know. I can sense when she's anxious. She shakes. She's shaking now."

"Oh," I say.

"She'll calm down," Hiroku says. "Why don't you hold her for a minute? I'll go get her supplies."

With that, she deposits the shaking bundle of fur into my arms.

I must look surprised by this, because Hiroku raises her brow. "You *are* prepared to care for her for the afternoon, correct? I have a meeting at four, and she can't miss her forest bathing."

"I -- um -- I wasn't exactly prepared to --" I stutter, as Blueberry Muffin starts squirming to get free. "I have a few other things going on --" I hug the shaking Chihuahua harder and begin petting her to try to get her to settle down.

Hiroku retrieves a thin change purse from her pocket, and starts pulling out bills. "How about I throw in an extra fifty dollars?" she says, holding a thick wad out towards me. "I'll give you the three hundred advance payment, plus another fifty. If you start today, that is."

My head bobs up and down, almost involuntarily as I reach for the bills with one hand. Maybe I'll get those cowboy boots after all!

"I guess I can push my other work back," I say, stuffing the bills into my bag. Blueberry is calming down a little bit. I feel her nuzzle her little chin against my shoulder.

It feels kind of good. She's very soft.

And cute.

And cuddly. More cuddly than I expected, actually.

Maybe I'm just a cat person because I've never had a dog.

Not a dog this cute, at least.

I barely notice that Hiroku has left us alone. Blueberry is licking my chin now.

When Hiroku returns, she has a strap-on baby carrier in one hand and sunglasses in the other.

She holds the pale pink baby carrier out to me. "It's all packed with everything you'll need," she says. "A water bottle, her no-rawhide chewy bones, her toothbrush, and her earmuffs." She pats the pockets as she speaks.

"If she's barking, it means that she's either thirsty or hungry. Try the bottle first, and then if that doesn't work, give her a treat. If she takes a treat, be sure to brush her teeth after. Of course, if she drinks water, you're going to need to give her a pee break. And if you happen to be anywhere with loud noise, please put the earmuffs on her."

Before I really know what's happening, Hiroku has bundled Blueberry into the carrier, on the front of my chest, and I'm threading my arms through the shoulder straps. Hiroku buckles the whole contraption at the back, and then tightens the straps. "How does that feel?" she asks.

"Um... good?" I say. I'm not sure how having a baby carrier loaded with a Chihuahua is *supposed* to feel. I wiggle my spine, as if assessing the fit of the carrier. "Yeah, that's good," I say again, as if all of this is normal.

Hiroku places the sunglasses over Blueberry's eyes. The glasses are tiny, and look like a cross between sunglasses and goggles. They fit with a strap around the little mutt's head.

"There," Hiroku says. "She absolutely can *not* go outside without her glasses. The sun is far too bright up here at altitude -- it could lead to macular degeneration if she's exposed."

"We don't want Blueberry to get macular degeneration," I say, even though I have only a vague idea of what that is.

"Not at all. Well, it looks like you're all set for a good session of forest bathing."

"Could you, maybe, explain to me what that is, exactly?" I ask.

Hiroku furrows her brow. "I thought you knew," she says.

"Not really," I admit.

"Shinrin-yoku," Hiroku says. "Forest bathing. You really haven't heard of it?"

I shake my head again.

"But you have a cat?" Hiroku asks.

I nod.

"A male, or a female?" asks Hiroku.

"A boy," I say.

"Well, how is his mental health?"

I consider Turkey's attitude of late. My furry roommate has been a little bit moody.

I hold out a hand and wave it back and forth. "So - so," I say.

She nods. "It's no wonder. If he's cooped up inside, he's missing out on the natural atmosphere of the forest. Trees are very healing for people and animals alike. Shinrin-yoku is the Japanese practice of spending time with trees. It's *essential* for mental health. Especially for animals."

"Oh," I say, guiltily thinking about all the time that Turkey spends indoors.

"Too many right angles are bad for the psyche," continues Hiroku. "Animals need to gaze out at organic shapes. "

"So how does it work?" I ask.

"I bring Blueberry out into the forest for at least two hours a day," Hiroku says. "All the research shows that it must be at least two hours out of every twenty-four. Blueberry and I usually go out from four to six. However, I've been so pressed for time lately." As if this reminds her of something, she glances at her watch.

When she speaks again, her words are more rushed. "Meetings, deadlines and such," she says. "That's where you come in. You'll be taking Blueberry out into the woods three times a week for her therapy."

"Got it," I say, as if this all makes perfect sense.

Hiroku seems to like my answer. She gives a curt nod, and then steps forward and kisses Blueberry Muffin on the nose.

As she backs up, she sends us off with a wave. "See you at six thirty," she says. "Meet me here!"

"Got it," I say again, since that response went over so well the first time.

With that, Blueberry and I head out the door.

Chapter Thirteen

With Blueberry strapped to my chest in a baby carrier, it's nearly impossible to ride my bike. I try it for at least a block, and nearly crash several times. I give up, and lock my bike to the bike rack in front of the library. Then, I begin hoofing it to my apartment by foot.

All this talk about pet care has me feeling like an awfully neglectful pet owner. Poor Turkey, cooped up in our little apartment all day, surrounded by right angles! Maybe he really does need some fresh air. I've decided to pick him up before heading out into the woods for my first forest bathing session.

We make it to the apartment and luckily, the door to unit B is closed, and there's no sign of Azure. I am sure she would have plenty to say about my current get-up, and I'm not sure all of it -- or any of it -- would be nice.

"Turkey?" I call out, as I open the door to my apartment. "I'm home! Want to go out for an outing?"

My eyes rove over the kitchen and then into the living room. Turkey is curled up on the couch, napping in a square of sunlight. At the sound of the door slamming closed behind me, he looks up sleepily.

"Hi!" I say, this time telepathically.

"Who is that?" Turkey asks.

"Meet Blueberry Muffin," I say. "I'm her nanny. We came home to see if you wanted to go for a walk with us."

"A walk?" Turkey's telepathic tone is a bit snooty, I must say.

"Yes. A walk. In the forest. I think you could use some fresh air."

"A *walk*," Turkey says. "With that thing?"

"She's a Chihuahua!" I say. I've walked over towards Turkey, and now I scoop him up.

Blueberry Muffin barks, and Turkey meows.

Both of them start squirming.

"Now, now," I say aloud. "Let's all be friends. Turkey, this is Blueberry Muffin. Blueberry, meet Turkey."

Blueberry barks. I might be imagining things, but I think it's a happy bark.

"Aw, Turkey, she likes you!" I say, as I hold my cat up to the carrier.

Is there room in this thing for both of them? I wonder, as I eye the carrier strapped to my chest. It *is* built for a human baby, and the little Chihuahua only weighs a couple of pounds. Turkey was the runt of his litter, and never grew to be very big.

Yes. I'm sure there's room in here for both of them.

Turkey is used to riding in my messenger bag, so this carrier shouldn't be too far of a stretch for him.

I begin loading him in.

"I am not going to ride in this thing with a dog!" Turkey transmits, haughtily, as I tuck his furry behind into the carrier.

"You'll like it," I tell him. "I promise. Just relax. Blueberry is really nice."

"She's a *dog*!" Turkey protests, still squirming.

Blueberry is yapping away happily. She's wiggling too.

"And you're a cat!" I tell Turkey.

"What's your point?" Turkey asks me.

"I don't know! What's yours? You said she's a dog like there's something wrong with that. There's nothing wrong with dogs, Turkey. Dogs are great."

"No, they aren't," Turkey says. "They slobber and drool and sniff each other's bottoms."

"Oh, don't be so judgmental. Just give her a chance." I can't believe I'm arguing with my cat.

I start walking towards the door, and on my way out I spot a pair of my sunglasses on the edge of the countertop. Marley gave them to me. They're oversized, with dark black lenses and red, green and yellow frames. Marley has a thing for Rastafarian colors.

I pick up the glasses and place them on Turkey. At first they slip off, so I undo my ponytail and use my hair tie to fasten the ends of the glasses together. When I put them on Turkey again, they stay on -- even when he shakes his head.

"You are torturing me!" Turkey complains as he uses a paw to try to get the glasses off.

"No, I'm not," I respond. "This is for your own good. You don't want to get macaroni generation, do you?

"Macaroni generation?" Turkey says. "What is that?"

I open the door, and step out onto the walkway. "Never mind," I say. "Just wear them. The sun is really bright up here at elevation. I promise you, it's better this way. We're going to be outside for two hours."

"Two hours!" Turkey moans.

"Three times a week," I tell him. "So get used to it."

"Can't I walk on my own?" Turkey asks. "I feel like a fool crammed into this carrier with a dog."

"Just relax, I say. You're going to like this, I promise."

As we begin walking down the stairs, Blueberry starts barking. These aren't just little 'yip yaps' sprinkled here and there. This is a full-blown cacophony of barking.

She must need something.

I stop at the bottom of the stairs, and begin opening pockets. I find the toothbrush first, and then the treats, but no bottle. The next pocket has the earmuffs in it.

"My ears!" Laments Turkey.

I pull out the earmuffs and place them on Turkey. They're bright pink, and fuzzy with fake fur.

"Better?" I ask.

"I suppose," Turkey answers.

I keep opening zippers, in a frenzy to find the bottle. Blueberries barking ricochets off every corrugated tin wall around me, and it sounds more like I'm standing amidst a *pack* of little lap dogs, not just with one.

Finally, I find the water bottle.

I hold it up in front of the dog's mouth, and she begins lapping at it.

"There, that's it," I say, as she drinks. "You were just thirsty, weren't you?"

I keep holding the bottle out in front of her as I start walking again.

"I think you dropped something," says a voice behind me.

Oh, *great*. Chris.

I turn and come face to face with Chris. He's holding up a bag of dog treats.

He jiggles them up and down. I feel myself blushing. "Yep, those are mine," I say.

"No-rawhide chew treats?" he asks. Then, he eyes the pet-daycare center I have taking place on my chest.

"Yup," I say. I'm not all that excited to tell Chris that I took on a new part time job. Also, I haven't seen him since he left my apartment the other night.

We both eye each other for a minute. He's waiting for an explanation about my get-up, and I'm not giving it.

"Did you… get a dog?" he asks.

"Something like that," I say.

"Okay," Chris blows out some air. "What's going on. Are you mad at me or something?"

"You didn't exactly leave on the best terms, last night," I say. "And I haven't heard from you since."

"And whose fault is that?" Chris asks. "You said you needed some time to think. I was giving you space."

I'm silent.

"Don't do this," he says. "Whenever things start to get even just a *little* bit serious between us, you pick a fight."

"Just a 'little bit' serious?" I say, raising my voice and flailing my arms. Drops of water squirt out of the bottle as I pull it free from Blueberry's mouth. "You said you might want to marry me!"

Some of the water lands on Chris's cheek, and he wipes it away.

"*Might*, Penny. I said, might. And what's wrong with that? When people date, it's usually because they enjoy being with the other person. Sometimes that leads to marriage."

I stay quiet. If I didn't have a zoo on my torso I would cross my arms over my chest. As it is, I jutt my hip out to the side.

Chris continues. "I'm thirty-one," he says. "Dating isn't just a game to me. I'm not saying I'm in a rush to get married or anything, I'm just saying I like thinking that it's a possibility."

"I don't want to talk about this!" I say. My heart is racing. "Chris, this really isn't a good time. I have alot on my mind."

"Penny, it's never a good time for you."

There's a silence between us again, and all that can be heard is a sucking sound as Blueberry licks the water bottle that I've returned to her lips.

"I really have work to do," I say. "Joe Gallant's niece Molly might have some information for me. Maybe she's been cleaning out his house and found a travel itinerary or something. Who knows?"

There's a knot in my stomach. I know I shouldn't be talking about work right now, but it seems a whole lot safer than talking about marriage -- with Christopher Wagner.

Chris sighs. "Right," he says. "Joe Gallant. That's what's important right now."

"What does that mean?" I ask. "It is! Melanie is missing, Chris. She didn't come home from her nail appointment, and the quiche she was supposed to bake got all sweaty on the counter!"

Chris looks at me like I'm crazy. I am waving my arms again, and I *have* dressed my cat in Rastafarian glasses and bright pink earmuffs. But I'm not crazy.

I just don't want to talk to Chris about our relationship, right now. Or ever.

"I know this scares you, Penny," Chris says, softly.

Gulp. He does?

He goes on. "How about this. I'll tell you how I feel, and you don't have to say anything."

I like the part about me not saying anything. I stand still, waiting for him to go on.

"Okay," Chris says, slowly. "I like you, Penny. Alot. I mean, *alot* alot. I liked you from the minute you entered police academy. You were funny, and nice, and smokin' hot. I remember you in high school too. You were always in the front row of the bleachers, cheering me on. I liked that."

Blueberry Muffin finally finishes drinking from the bottle, and I let my arm fall. I'm captivated by Chris' words. Smokin' hot? *Me*? I wait for him to say more.

He does. "When I'm with you, time seems to fly by. When I'm not with you, I'm thinking about you. I messed up, all those years ago… and I'm not going to let that happen again."

I swallow, hard. My throat feels dry and parched. I have half a mind to yank out Blueberry's water bottle and take a sip for myself.

Chris isn't talking anymore. He said that I didn't need to talk, but now I feel like he's waiting for me to reply.

How can I respond to that?

My younger self would be doing summersaults right now, flipping out that Christopher Wagner was this into me. But I'm older now. More mature -- I guess you could say. I've lived through a breakup with Chris, and I won't allow myself to let the sun rise and fall with him again. Then there's the fact that I'm becoming someone brand new, the more I learn about the magical abilities that I possess.

Chris steps backwards, and then to the side. He's moving around me. I can't let him go, without saying *something*.

I clear my throat.

He stops moving.

"Chris -- that's really flattering," I say. "I mean it. A few years ago, I would have died on the spot if you told me that." I laugh, nervously.

Chris doesn't join in.

"And I like you too," I say. "I really do. We have so much fun together. But --" Oh, goodness, this is hard to say.

I swallow, and clear my throat again. Chris looks just as uncomfortable as I feel. "But -- we're really different, Chris."

I can almost hear Max's words, playing through my mind: *'Humans and magical beings don't make good couples.'*

I avoid Chris's eyes as I continue. "We've always been different, Chris, but now we are, more than ever."

I can't bring myself to tell him that I'm now practicing witchcraft. I just can't. Not now.

Chris hangs his head. He begins nodding. "Okay," he says. "Okay. I'm glad we're talking about this. I guess this is what I wanted. To talk."

I bite my lip.

"Well," he says, lifting his head. "It's good to know how you feel. I -- I *like* how different we are. I didn't know it was a problem for you."

"It's not a problem," I mumble.

"It *sounds* like it is," Chris says.

I sigh. "I don't want to stop hanging out with you," I say. "But it's best if it's just casual right now."

He shakes his head. "Penny, I don't know if I can do 'casual' for much longer. Not with you. I like you too much. I can't pretend otherwise"

"Then where does that leave us?" I ask.

He looks sad. Really sad. I hate this.

With wide eyes, he says, "I guess, if we're going to do this, I want to know that you're all in. *I'm* all in, Penny. You know how I feel about you. I want to know that you feel the same way."

I feel my eyes widen too. This is happening. This discussion went so much deeper than I expected it to or wanted it to. Part of me knew it was coming, but that didn't stop me from avoiding it like the plague.

I'm frozen. Petrified. Unable to speak.

Chris is backing away from me. "Think it over," he says.

Then, he's gone.

Turkey's voice emanates through my mind. "Thank goodness that's over," he says. "That was painfully awkward. Will you get these muffs off my ears? They're driving me crazy."

I reach for the earmuffs. I feel like I'm operating on autopilot. Though my arms are moving, I'm not conscious of anything except the lingering energy of my conversation with Chris.

Did we just break up?

Have I just pushed him so far away that I won't be able to get him back, if I want him?

Do I want him?

My questions overwhelm me, and as I tuck the earmuffs and the dog treats Chris handed me back into their zipped compartments, I struggle to regain a sense of control.

Yes, my relationship with Chris feels overwhelming at this moment, but there are other things in my life that I'm *totally* on top of.

Like the little fur balls under my care. I can take them out into the forest and Shinrin egg yolk the heck out of this afternoon.

And before that, I might even squeeze in a quick bit of detective work.

Molly Gallants house is right in the middle of town, right on my way towards a bunch of trails I could choose to take into the forest. I could stop-by to ask her some questions on my way out into the woods.

Ha! Look at me. A detective *and* a dog nanny. Totally on top of things.

Without another thought about Chris and his big, blue-grey eyes, I march off in the direction of Molly Gallant's house.

Chapter Fourteen

I walk so fast, due to my anxiety and frustration over what's just happened with Chris, that I make it to Molly Gallant's house surprisingly quick. The baby carrier *and* my messenger bag make me feel like a pack horse as I hustle along, and I find myself wishing more than once that I was whizzing along on my bike. I stop to catch my breath once I reach Molly's front gate.

Molly's house is pink, with purple shutters. The 'picket fence' around her yard is made of old skis. I spot Molly's rusty, yellow town cruiser on her front porch, which makes me hopeful that she is home.

I make my way up her walkway, and flinch when a giant German shepherd starts going bonkers inside. He's jumping up and down in front of the window, just off to one side of the door. His jumps are so high that he almost looks like he's bouncing on a trampoline.

I'm hoping that he won't come tearing out of the house when Molly opens the door, but just in case I ready myself to run as I reach up to knock. My body is positioned for a sprint back down the walkway, in case the German shepherd should come after us. I can feel Blueberry Muffin quake a little bit each time the beast within the house barks.

After a few minutes of tense waiting, Molly comes to the door. I hear her yelling at the dog before she opens up, and then she squeezes through the door and out to the front stoop, without letting her dog free. Thank goodness!

She's wearing a tie dye shirt and ripped jeans, with a blue apron over the top. The last I knew, Molly was teaching ceramics at the art co-op in town. By the looks of her outfit, she's also working on her art from home.

"Sorry about that," she says. "Charlie is still a puppy. Visitors make him excited. He also likes to chase cats, so…" she eyes Turkey, who is just visible by the tips of his ears, because he's cowering so far within the baby carrier.

"Do you see why I like to stay indoors?" Turkey asks me, telepathically. "That thing could eat me in two bites."

"I'm sure Charlie wouldn't eat you," I respond mentally.

I'm not sure.

Molly wipes her hands on her apron. Streaks of gray clay form fingerprints on the blue fabric. "What's up?" she asks. "Is this some kind of outreach visit from the animal shelter? I didn't know you volunteered there, Penny."

"No," I say. "I know I *look* like I work at the animal shelter right now, but I'm actually visiting as a private investigator."

"Oh. Is this about the art co-op? I totally *thought* I locked up, but I must have forgotten. Otherwise, I don't know *how* that homeless guy could have gotten in there. I know I should have called the cops, but I was --"

"It's not about the art co-op," I say, cutting her off. "I'm actually here to talk to you about your uncle."

"Oh." Her face falls.

"I'm so sorry about his passing," I say.

"Thanks. It was really unexpected." She wraps her arms around her torso, giving herself a hug.

"You're his next of kin, right?" I ask.

She nods.

"Have you been cleaning out his house?" I ask.

"Yeah... why?" Now she gives me a funny look. "Why do you care about his house?"

"Look," I say. "I don't know anything for certain, but I have the idea that foul play may have been involved in your uncle's death."

"What? Why do you think that?" Molly asks. "Uncle Joe was a good guy. Everyone loved him!"

I open my mouth to speak, but before I can, Molly says, "What are the police doing about this?"

"Hold on," I say.

I wait a minute for her to calm down. Charlie is still going bonkers inside, which isn't very helpful in creating a calming environment. Despite my beat of silence, I can tell Molly is still struggling to process what I've just told her.

"It's just a theory," I say. "Like I said, I don't know for sure. The police are pretty sure it was an accident. But some things have been coming to light -- related to another case -- that are making me think otherwise. If I can collect some evidence to prove that foul play is involved, then the police will have to open up an investigation. That's why I'm here."

"Good," Molly says. "If someone killed my Uncle, I want to know."

"Then you'll help me with something?" I ask.

"Anything," Molly says.

"I need to know if you found any travel itineraries or flight confirmations, when you were going through Joe's stuff," I say. "Maybe from a company called Express Travel?"

Molly thinks this over, but then shakes her head. "Not that I can think of," she says. "Uncle Joe didn't have a lot of papers around. I think he took care of most of his business -- you know, bills and that kind of thing -- on his phone."

"Do you have his phone?" I ask.

She nods.

"Could I borrow it?" I ask. "I'd like to check out his emails. It would also be helpful to see the calls that he made."

Molly hesitates. "That seems awfully private," she says. "I don't' know if he'd want someone looking through all that."

"Would he want his killer to get away with murder?" I ask.

This does it. "I'll be right back," Molly says.

There's another tense moment when she opens the door. I think Turkey, Blueberry Muffin and I all half expect Charlie to come bolting out. He does try, but Molly catches him by the collar. "Oh, no you don't!" she says.

The three of us exhale a collective sigh of relief when the door closes, once again barricading Charlie inside. A few minutes later, Molly squeezes through, and steps back out onto the porch. In her hands is a black cellphone.

"Here you go," she says, holding it out to me. "I'd like it back, when you're done."

"No problem," I say, as I tuck the phone into my messenger bag.

"The password is pretty easy," Molly says, as I work to arrange the many straps that I have crossing my body. "Five-five-five-five. I bet you can't guess what my uncle's lucky number was!"

"Five?" I say.

Molly chuckles. Then she becomes somber again. "Keep me updated, okay? And if there's anything I can do to help…"

"I'll let you know," I promise. Then, patting my bag I add, "This phone is a great start. Thank you."

As I retreat down the walkway and the sound of German shepherd barking fades, I feel Blueberry muffin stop quivering. Turkey's head pops up from within the carrier.

"Sorry about that, guys," I say.

Blueberry Muffin yips twice. "And ladies," I add. She licks my chin.

I lean down and kiss the top of her little head.

Turkey shoots me a glare, over his shoulder.

"Don't be jealous," I say aloud.

"I'm not jealous," he responds within my mind. "I just thought you had better taste, that's all."

"Come on, Turkey, you've got to admit that she's cute," I say telepathically.

Turkey says nothing. As we walk along, I pull the phone from the pocket I tucked it into. It's harder than I thought to try to work the phone *and* carry two animals, so I pause next to a stone wall under the shade of a tree.

Blueberry gets all wiggly as soon as we stop. "What is it?" I ask. Then, thinking about all the water she's just ingested, I take a guess. "Do you have to pee?"

She answers with a sharp bark.

I pull her from the carrier, and Turkey gives a happy sigh. "Now *this* is more like it," he says spreading out in the carrier.

"Don't get too used to it," I warn him.

Blueberry Muffin starts exploring the ground around the stonewall, looking for a place to relieve herself.

As she does her business, I take the opportunity to start digging through Joe's phone. Taking a seat on the cool stones, I start scrolling.

First, I open his email inbox. It's fairly crowded with junk mail and fantasy football league notices, so I enter in a quick search for 'Hawaii'. Immediately, a result pops up.

I open it.

Express Travel Confirmation and Receipt for:
Joseph Gallant
Destination: Oahu, Hawaii
Flight information:
Departure: Flight A1665 Departing Denver at 3:05 pm on August 15, 2018

You have no return flight booked for this trip.

Joseph, your flight is confirmed! Your confirmation number is 810995

Please be sure to check in online at expresstravel.com for boarding prior to your trip.

My eyes nearly bulge out of my head. This flight information looks eerily familiar!

Rummaging in my bag, I find the printed piece of paper that Cliff handed me. I scan Melanie's travel confirmation, to find that the flight information is indeed identical to Joe's.

I stop reading, and stuff the paper and phone back into my bag. I've seen enough, and plus, Blueberry is pawing at my bare leg, and it doesn't feel pleasant.

"Did you do your business?" I ask, before bending down to scoop her up.

"Careful!" Turkey says, as I stoop over and he almost spills out of the carrier.

"Sorry," I say. "I'm not used to this thing, and I'm a little bit distracted. Joe Gallant was going to go to Hawaii, with Melanie! On the same flight and everything! It was a date."

"Melanie Haywater, the mayor's wife?" Turkey asks.

"Yes," I say, as I begin lowering Blueberry into the carrier. "Turkey, you're going to have to make some room for her."

Reluctantly, Turkey rearranges himself. "What does that mean, for your case?" he asks.

"I'm not sure," I answer. "If Melanie and Joe were going to jet off to Hawaii together, Melanie certainly wouldn't have killed him. She just picked up clothes for their big vacation. She was excited about it."

"Oahu is a very romantic destination," Turkey says. "They must have been in love."

I agree with my cat. "It sounds like they were going to celebrate Melanie's divorce in style." Then I have an idea. "What if Cliff found out about it?" I say.

"That could have upset him," Turkey says. "I'm no detective, but I did read all of your Speedy's course material. I'd venture to say that's enough motive for murder."

"Yes," I reply. "But then why would Cliff come to me? That makes no sense. The police already wrote off Joe's death, so it would be like he was getting away with...well... murder, really. There would be no reason for him to come to my office and start raising red flags."

"No, you're right," Turkey says.

It's nice to agree with him, for once.

I pat his head, and he starts to purr. I maneuver myself up to a standing position, which is a bit tricky due to all the baggage that I'm carrying. Before I begin walking, I pull Joe's phone from my bag and look at it again.

"Guys," I say aloud.

Blueberry yips once. "And ladies," I add, before she can bark again.

She settles down.

I continue, "We're just going to hang out here for a second while I check out Joe's calls, really quickly. Then we'll hit the trails."

I feel Blueberry give a happy squirm.

When I start looking through Joe's calls, the first thing I note is that there are none from Melanie. The two must have been very careful about their communication. They *must* have talked, given that they booked the same exact flight, for goodness sake, but I see no calls from her, and I also saw no emails.

The second item of interest doesn't jump out at me until I've scrolled back to the fourteenth of August -- the day that Joe died.

I see zero calls.

Nothing. No outgoing calls, and more importantly, no incoming calls.

"Ah ha!" I say, as I return the phone to my bag's pocket.

"What did you figure out?" Asks Turkey.

"There are no incoming calls, from the day that Joe died."

"And?" Turkey prompts.

"And that means that I was right -- Ralph *is* lying. He lied to me, and he lied to Glenn."

"Do explain," Turkey says.

"Well, Ralph said he went straight to the restaurant's office and stayed there all morning and assumed that Joe was in the kitchen working with Glenn. But *Glenn* said that Ralph came out of the office and reported that Joe wasn't coming in to work. Ralph even said that he tried to call Joe."

"But the phone proves that Ralph never called," says Turkey.

"Right," I say.

"But couldn't *Glenn* be lying?" Turkey asks.

Technically, my cat is right. But something deep inside of me tells me otherwise.

"He could be," I say, "but I don't think he is. My money's on Ralph."

"Why?" Turkey asks.

"Call it witchy intuition," I say.

Turkey accepts this answer. After all, he's been reading ASBW lately, just as much as I have. "Okay," he says. "So you think Ralph was lying. What are you going to do about it?"

"Well, I say, it's time to do some forest bathing."

"So you're just going to forget about the case, when you've just made so much progress?" Turkey asks. He sounds disappointed.

"No," I say. "I'm not going to forget about it. I didn't tell you *where* we're going to do our forest bathing, did I?"

"No, you did not," Turkey answers.

"We're going to soak up the trees while we walk up the long and well-wooded path to Rainbow Lake, on which Ralph just happens to have a cabin."

"I see," says Turkey. Now he sounds very pleased.

"I want to see the place," I say. "It will be a nice hike, too."

"Sure," replies Turkey. "You're really going there for the hike. It has *nothing* to do with the case, does it?"

I smile. It's good to know that sarcasm works, even with telepathy.

Within ten minutes, we reach the beginning of the hike.

I've hiked on the path up to Rainbow Lake many times. The trailhead is right behind the library, and it is a nice mellow hike in the beginning, so I've wandered on it with Marley when we want to catch up but don't feel like cruising around town in her van, sitting at the Death Cafe, or hanging out in my apartment.

It's one of those hikes that lends itself to talking and walking. Nice and wide, with very little actual climbing.

In the beginning, at least.

Tonight, with my animals snuggled in the carrier, I charge past the place where Marley and I usually turn around.

The signs still point to Rainbow Lake, but the terrain gets rockier, and steeper. The incline is made more challenging due to the extra weight I'm carrying, not to mention the ongoing commentary from one of my charges.

"Watch out for that rock!" Turkey says, as I make my way up a windy section of the trail.

"Dude, there are literally hundreds of rocks on the ground," I reply mentally. "It's impossible for me to tell which one you mean."

Just then, I trip over a particularly obstructive rock, and just barely catch myself before landing on my face. *Our* faces, I should say, because my fall would pretty much bring all three to the dirt.

"*That* one," Turkey says, as I try to catch my breath.

"Thanks", I say sarcastically.

"No problem," Turkey responds. "And please don't call me dude."

"Why not?" I ask.

"We are not on a ranch, are we Penelope? If we were on a ranch, then dude would be an appropriate word to use. As it is, I'd appreciate it if you didn't use it. It's already hard for me to go by Turkey."

"You know," I say. "This walk would be alot easier going if you weren't complaining the whole time."

"I'm not complaining! I'm giving you pointers. Like watch out for that branch!"

"What br--" I stop the thought in my head as a branch slaps me in the face.

"Got it," I say. "Next time, a little more warning in advance would be good."

"I would have given you more warning, if I'd seen it earlier, but -- Penelope, what's that hanging from the branch?"

I'm now carefully sidestepping the offending tree limb, and as Turkey transmits this to me, I look over at it.

"It looks like another hiker lost a shirt," I say. "Maybe they had it tied around their waist or something, and it snagged on the branch. This branch *is* like right in the middle of the trail."

I walk over to the shirt, and pull it off the twigs that it's caught on.

"Hang on. This shirt looks familiar!" I say, staring at the frilly design. "You know what? I've seen Melanie wearing it before, at Zumba. I recognize it because she is the only woman who practically dresses up for class. Not what I'd want to wear to a sweat-session, but to each his own, I suppose."

I hold the shirt up to my nose. It even *smells* like Melanie. She's always wearing an overpowering perfume.

"Blech!" says Turkey. "That smells awful."

Blueberry Muffin, who up until now has been gazing around at the trees blissfully, with her tongue lolling out to the side, now yips several times in a row.

I hold the shirt out as far as I can, pinching it between my pointer finger and thumb. "Okay, okay," I say. "I get it! It stinks. But this is a clue!"

"Melanie was here," Turkey says.

"Recently," I add. "The scent of her perfume has barely faded."

"Unfortunately," Turkey adds.

I toss the shirt to the side, and keep hiking, fast. Suddenly, a feeling of urgency fills me. What was Melanie doing up here -- *today*, by the smell of things?

Cliff said that she was missing. The fact that she hiked this very trail, very recently, can't just be a coincidence.

I get chills just thinking about it. Or, these goosebumps might just be due to the dropping temperatures. Now that it's past five, and we're in the cold woods, I'm wishing I had a jacket of some sort.

Since the woods provide some shade from the trees, I remove the glasses from the animals. I notice now, that not only is it shady, but it's actually getting quite dark. The sun must be setting behind the mountains across the valley, leaving our box canyon and much of the hillsides in deep shadows.

What time is it, anyways? I wonder, as I embark upon another staircase like stretch of the trail. I know it's past five, but how far past five?

I pause long enough to take out my phone. A quick glance at my screen tells me that it's almost five-thirty.

I also see that I have two new text messages.

One is from Hiroku. *'How is everything going?'* it says.

The second is from Chris. *'Am I going to see you tonight?'* he asks.

I don't know how to answer him. After typing out a quick 'great!' to Hiroku, I jam my phone back into my bag, wishing that I'd never taken it out.

Because now that I've seen his text, all I can do is think about Chris.

He said that he likes me. Alot. Actually, he said that he likes me *alot* alot.

I smile, thinking of it.

Then, my smile fades. How am I ever going to tell him about *The Art and Science of Being a Witch*?

How could I tell him that I'm becoming something new? Something other. Something different. Something inhuman.

Max said that humans and magical beings shouldn't date, and I understand what he means, now that it's happening to me. One day, I won't be human at all, not even a part of me. I'll become purely magical -- like Max and Azure.

They don't identify as human, because they're not.

But Christopher Wagner will always be human. I know this, at a gut level.

"You have two options," Turkey says, within my mind.

"Wait!" I reply. "You could hear my thoughts?"

"I'm an extension of you -- remember?" Turkey says. "We're not just communicating when we use *words* like this. We're always going to be energetically intertwined. I can tell what you're feeling."

"Oh." I guess privacy really isn't a part of being a witch, I think. "What are my two options?" I say.

Without hesitation, Turkey replies. "Either you share everything with him, and take the risk that he will no longer love you, or --"

"Hold on!" I transmit. "No one said anything about love."

"Christopher Wagner loves you, and you know it," Turkey says. "He basically said it today."

"No! He said he likes me, *alot* alot," I protest.

"That's jock-language for love," Turkey says. "Neither of you are very good at communicating, but Christopher is *especially* bad at talking about his feelings. However, at least he's trying. Unlike *someone*...."

"I tried!" I say. Then I ask, "So, if I tell him I'm learning to be a witch, he might not love me anymore?"

"You know this is true," Turkey says. "Magic frightens some people. Chris may react unfavorably to your abilities."

"I know," I say. The trees are growing thinner as we climb, and now I start to spot more visible sky between the scraggly branches. I think we're nearing the top. It's a good thing, because seeing as it's now five thirty, I'm fairly certain that we're going to be late to meet Hiroku at the law office. But we can't turn back now.

I continue on, towards the clearing. "What's the other option?" I ask, because option one isn't sounding all that good to me.

"You could hide it from him, and always keep the magical part of your life a secret."

"Just pretend I'm normal?" I ask.

"Well, not normal," Turkey says. "But yes, just pretend you're plain old Penny Banks -pre-magical abilities. You'll be the girl he fell in love with... forever."

"But I'll never feel truly honest," I say. "I'll always be holding back."

"Both options entail possible sacrifice," says Turkey.

I push past the last clingy branches, and the three of us emerge onto a clearing. There's a sparkling blue lake, spread out before us. It glitters in the fading light, perfectly reflecting the peach-tinted clouds and surrounding trees. Off to one side, I spot a weathered grey cabin.

"How am I going to decide which option to go with?" I ask my cat.

"If I knew, I would tell you," promises Turkey. "But I'm a part of you, remember? You're truly undecided. Only time will tell."

"You know, Max says time isn't as linear as humans think it is?" I say.

"Do explain," Turkey responds.

We're moving towards the cabin now. There are little clusters of trees, every few feet away and I find myself half jogging from one cluster to the next as we near the cabin. I want to be hidden from the view, but I'm not sure why. It's just this nervous feeling I have.

Maybe it's because it's so eerily quiet up here, and I know that Ralph could be a murderer.

Whatever it is, it's filling me with a spooky sense of trepidation. I can barely focus on the discussion I'm having with Turkey. However, talking with him in my mind is keeping me calm, so as I scurry to an even closer clump of trees, I attempt to continue.

"Max says that --"

I'm interrupted by a sound that transforms my mild trepidation into terror: a woman's scream pierces through the clearing, causing birds to abandon their perches, and take flight into the sky.

Who was that? I think, as my heart leaps to my throat.

Melanie?

I run faster, darting from one group of trees to the next. Soon, I'm just five feet from the cabin. I can see a window.

I'm about to move in closer, when there's another scream.

It's a blood curdling shriek, filled with terror. This is no yell of surprise or happiness. Someone -- a woman, by the sounds of it -- is screaming as if her life depended on it.

The sound pulsates from the cabin, vibrating through the twilight air.

Suddenly, the scream is joined by another sound.

Yip, yip, yip!

The scream dies down, and Blueberry Muffin gives one last little *yip*.

"Shhh!" I say, reaching around the Chihuahua's snout and pressing my hand against her lips.

She begins licking my hand. I start to retreat, as quickly as I can. I bounce backwards, trying to put as much space between myself and the creepy cabin as possible.

The clearing is perfectly quiet once again. The scream has stopped echoing off the rocky mountains that surround the clearing, and Blueberry's barks have faded as well.

Maybe whoever was inside, didn't notice.

Now that I'm farther away, I crouch down behind a large boulder. I wait, with my back pressed against the cold rock. I'm breathing hard. My one hand is still in front of Blueberry's snout, and her little warm tongue is lapping away at my fingers.

At least if she's licking me, she's not barking.

While she's still licking my fingers, I use my other hand to begin pulling the shoulder straps of the carrier off me.

"What are you doing?" Turkey asks me.

"You have to stay here, with Blueberry Muffin," I say. "I'm going to go see what's happening in that cabin."

"Someone's screaming in there, that's what's happening!" Turkey says. He sounds a bit panicked. That makes sense, because he's an extension of me, and *I'm* a bit panicked.

I reach around my back and fumble with the buckles until I feel them release.

"I have to go see what's going on," I say. "What if it's Melanie in there? What if she's hurt?"

"Don't leave us here!" Turkey pleads.

"Turkey," I say, stroking his head and then scratching behind his ears. "You can do this. Just watch over Blueberry. It could be dangerous in that cabin, and I don't want you two in harm's way."

"But I don't want *you* in harm's way either!" protests Turkey. "You can't go over there. It's not safe!"

"I have to," I repeat.

Nervously, I pull my messenger bag off my shoulder. I search through it and find my gun. Next, I find the handcuffs. The key is inserted in the lock, and I remove it, and slide it into a small pocket in my bag.

If I'm desperate enough to use these cuffs, I won't be needing the key right away. I make sure that the cuffs are in a loaded position, and then push them into the back pocket of my black pants.

"Be careful," Turkey says, as he watches me prepare.

I feel like a warrior, about to charge into battle. I lean down and kiss Turkey on the nose. Then, because I'm feeling truly scared, I kiss Blueberry too.

Seeing Turkey's jealous expression, I finish with one more kiss on his nose.

"I'll be back," I promise, giving him one last scratch behind his ears.

Then, I turn and begin running towards the cabin with my gun drawn.

Chapter Fifteen

As I approach the cabin, I hear someone shouting.

I recognize Melanie Haywater's voice. "I'm going to tell *everyone* what you've done!" she says. "You're not going to get away with this!"

I move faster.

I've never been a runner, but my adrenaline has kicked me so far into 'fight or flight' gear that I feel like I could win the Hillcrest one-mile Dash for A Cure, if it was happening right now.

I'm not even conscious of the steps I'm taking. My feet seem to move effortlessly over the rock-strewn ground, and in an instant, I'm at the cabin's door.

I don't knock. Instead, I barge right in, waving my gun. "Stop!" I shout, though I have no idea what I might be stopping.

I see Melanie tied up in a chair. There's a cinder block strapped to her feet. Her cheeks are tear stained. Her eye fly open wide at the sight of me.

"Penny, behind you!" she says.

I begin to whirl around, but it's too late. I feel the impact of a body smashing into me, and strong, wiry arms wrap around my torso.

Like a football player being tackled, I begin flying to the ground. As the cabin's rustic wood floor zooms up to my face, I squeeze my eyes shut. In another split second, my right cheek thuds against the hard floor, followed soundly by my forehead. There's a body on top of me.

"I knew I heard something out there," says the body. Though my eyes are closed, I know that smug, sleazy voice. It's Ralph!

"Get off me!" I shout.

"Or what are you going to do?" Ralph says.

I feel my gun, still in my hand, being pried away from me. I open my eyes just in time to see it slide across the floor, out of reach.

"Shoot me?" Ralph finishes.

Then, I feel my hands being tied roughly behind my back, with scratchy, thick rope.

Shoot. This is not going well. At all.

I'm on my stomach, pinned flat to the ground. My arms are now tied.

My legs are still free! I start kicking.

"Oh, no you don't!" Ralph says. This is when I feel his efforts move to my ankles. He grabs for one foot, and then the other, and then I feel the rope bind my legs together.

"That pinches!" I say, as he secures the knot.

"Don't worry, it won't hurt for long," he says smugly. I cringe at his words. I don't like the sound of them.

"What -- are you going to kill me, like you killed Joe Gallant?" I ask.

I feel Ralph's hands, which have been working with the knot, still for a moment. I've affected him.

Encouraged, I keep talking. "You can't stuff me in a freezer, up here, Ralph. I'm not going to freeze to death, like Joe did."

"He's going to *drown* us!" Melanie says. She's crying, and her voice is ragged. "He said he was going to take me out in his rowboat and throw me over the side. *Do something, Penny!*"

Now the cinderblock tied to her feet makes sense.

I speak. "Melanie figured it out first, didn't she, Ralph? When I started poking around, saying that Joe's death wasn't an accident, Melanie caught on fast. She figured out that you did it, before I did!"

"What you said that day, when you came for coffee, made so much sense," Melanie says tearfully. "The freezer never malfunctioned before. Why would it, on the day that the restaurant was to be sold?"

"How did you know it was Ralph?" I ask her.

I feel Ralph's bodyweight lift off me. I'm still on my stomach, but as he gets up I'm able to roll onto my back. Then, with a heroic abdominal effort that I think Jumper Strongheart would have been proud of, I manage to sit.

Melanie is speaking. "I've always had a bad feeling about Ralph," Melanie says. "And when I came up here to talk to him, just today, he went bezerk. He tied me up -- that's enough of an admission of guilt for me."

"It is for me, too," I say.

"Stop it!" Ralph shouts.

He's moves across the room, to where Melanie is seated. He begins dragging her chair towards the door. "You both think you are so clever! Tell it to the fishes."

"Why did you do it, Ralph?" I ask. "Did you hate Joe so much that passion drove you to end his life, or was it a strategic move, to ensure you would own the restaurant?"

I can see his face clearly now, as he works to move Melanie across the room. He grimaces as he strains against the weight of her body, the chair, and the cinder block.

My hands are behind me, but if I make fists, I can use them as leverage against the floor. I press my hands into the ground and try to move my hips. It works! I've moved a few inches to the right.

If I can cut Ralph off at the door, maybe I could stop him.

I repeat the reverse-crab walk kind of move. Again, I use my hands to press into the ground, lift my hips up, and swing them to the right.

"Hey! Stop that!" Ralph says, looking over at me. He's really struggling to move Melanie's chair, and when he pauses to look at me, he's out of breath.

"Why did you do it, Ralph?" I ask again.

I can see that we're flustering him. He's losing some of his suave sleaziness. He's beginning to look overwhelmed. I move again towards the door.

"Stop that!" he shouts, abandoning Melanie's chair and approaching me. "Stop moving like that, or I'll kill you right here and now!" He points to my gun, on the floor on the other end of the cabin, where he threw it.

"I don't think you would, Ralph. That's not your style," I say. I crab-walk again, just to test him.

He moves towards my gun.

I hope I'm right about this.

I keep talking as he stoops to pick up the gun. "You're not a murderer, Ralph. You just want to be successful. You want to have friends. You want to be liked. You thought owning the restaurant would get you there. You didn't hate Joe, did you? You didn't even *want* to kill him."

He picks up the gun. His brow is furrowed. "I *had* to kill him," he says. "Cliff would have given the restaurant to him, if I didn't. I would have been Cliff's assistant for the rest of my life. This was my only chance at something better."

"It was easy to do, once Joe was in the freezer," I say. "You just closed the door, turned down the temperature, and made sure that he couldn't get out. It was like you weren't even killing him."

Ralph aims the gun at me. His hand is unsteady. This is really getting to him.

"You're not going to shoot me, Ralph," I say, trying to keep my voice even. "That would be far too violent. Too messy. That's why you put Joe in the freezer, and why you want to drown us. If it looks like an accident, you can convince yourself that it *was* an accident."

"You both could have come up here, for a paddle in the lake," Ralph says, lowering the gun. "I'll untie you once you're at the bottom. I'll leave the boat, drifting out of the water. When your bodies are found, the town will mourn your tragic *accidental* death."

"It's still murder," I say. "Someone will find out."

"Who?" Ralph asks.

Now that he's set the gun down, he's walking towards a small closet next to the cabin's little kitchen area. I watch him open the closet door, and bend down to reach into what looks like a tool box. When he crosses the room, heading in my direction, I see a roll of duct tape in his hands.

He pulls off about a foot of the silver tape, and tears it with his teeth.

"I think I've heard enough from you," he says.

I try out my crab-walk maneuver, but this time I don't get very far. Ralph stoops over me, and places the tape over my mouth.

Then, he scoops his hand under my arm, and drags me up to my feet. I let my body go limp, hoping that dead weight will be harder for him to drag along. However, the little man is surprisingly strong.

He maneuvers me into a wooden chair, and then wraps a rope around my torso, half a dozen times. At first, I rock back and forth while screaming, despite the tape, as he works. The scream is muffled, and the more rope that gets coiled around me, the less wiggle room I have for rocking. Soon, I'm not even able to move an inch.

"Penny!" Melanie shouts. "Penny, keep fighting him! He's a no-good-weasel of a man! He's not going to get away with this. Ralph, you absolute coward! You rotten --"

Ralph bounds over to Melanie, and I watch as he stops her words short by applying duct tape to her mouth.

He stands up straight.

Melanie and I are both screaming, but with the tape over our mouths, our cries are muffled and wordless.

"That's better," Ralph says, tossing the roll of duct tape away from him and then brushing his hands together, as if he just completed a particularly challenging home repair project.

He continues dragging Melanie, in her chair, to the cabin door. I watch in horror as he unties her torso, so that she's free from the chair. Her arms and legs are bound, like mine are. He hoists her, fireman style, over one shoulder. Though she's petite, she does have a cinderblock strapped to her feet, and he strains against the weight.

As Ralph reaches the threshold of the door, with a squirming, squealing-beneath-the-tape Melanie over his shoulder, he turns to me. "Don't move," he warns.

In protest, I start wiggling, as much as I can. When I rock side to side, I feel the chair begin to move with me. Suddenly, the whole chair tips over. The side of my head smacks against the floor. It hurts.

"I *said*, don't move!" Ralph says.

My vision is skewed. The world has turned sideways. I see Ralph put Melanie on the floor, as if she's a sack of potatoes. Then he walks towards me, and disappears around the back of the chair.

I feel the chair being righted, and then he's dragging me across the cabin, towards the kitchen and the little closet that I noticed earlier.

I struggle as much as I can, but no matter what I do, I can't stop him from dragging the chair, with me tied to it, into the closet.

"I'll be back for you," he says ominously.

He slams the closet door closed, and I hear him lock it.

Everything turns pitch black. I can't see a single thing.

The sound of Melanie's struggle fades quickly. I can picture the rowboat that I saw along the shore. It's a ways away from the cabin -- it will take Ralph some time to get there.

I have time.

I have to get free.

But how?

There's panic rising in my chest, and my thoughts are racing. I strain my eyes, trying to make them adjust to the darkness faster.

It's no use.

Sweat beads form on my forehead, and my breath comes out in short, hot bursts from my nostrils. Each time I try to suck air in, I feel like I'm getting less and less.

If I keep this up, I'm going to hyperventilate and pass out, and then I *really* won't have a shot at saving Melanie. Or myself.

I squeeze my eyes shut and slow my breathing. As I slow my breathing, time itself seems to slow down. I focus on the sensation of air moving through my nose; in and out, in and out.

Slowly. Slowly.

My heart, which has been galloping within my chest, begins to slow down too.

Breathe, I tell myself. In and out.

My world is dark. As I focus on my breathing, everything else begins to fade from my awareness -- the cabin, the rowboat, the cinder block around Melanie's ankles.

The steely grey sky, the peach clouds, the glittering lake of ice-cold mountain water. The trees, the trail down to town, it all fades.

Even Hillcrest begins to fade from my awareness. The constant background hum of people and their needs, desires, and concerns slips, dissolves, and then evaporates completely.

All I am aware of is the air, moving gently over the space just below my nostrils.

My reality is pinpointed on this one sensation.

In darkness and silence, I feel myself enter a state of complete tranquility.

Though my eyes are closed, and I'm in a pitch-black closet, I start to see shapes.

They are clouds.

I feel as if I am above them, flying almost. I'm reminded of my dream, in which I was soaring above puffy white clouds. As I think of my dream, the vision becomes stronger.

It's like I can *see* the clouds.

Then, a voice enters my consciousness. It's just like when I hear Turkey's voice, in my mind, except this time it's not Turkey's voice that I hear.

The voice is as clear as a bell -- neither male nor female. "Your place of power is above the clouds. You can only get there with solitude and silence," the voice says.

As the voice speaks, I feel warmth in my chest, and I think of my necklace. The Power Spell! It is activating. I know this in the core of my being. I feel the warm sensation spread to my toes, fingers, and up to my scalp.

I'm not afraid -- not even one little, tiny bit. I feel completely safe, secure, and almost giddy with joy, despite my dire circumstances. As the warmth fills my body, I open my eyes.

I see a crack of light beneath the door. I wiggle, trying to sense how tightly the ropes are wrapped around me. They're tight. As I move, the chair squeaks and groans. It's an old, wooden chair, fairly lightweight.

I put pressure on my feet, and manage to rock forward until I'm almost standing, though my knees are bent.

With as much force as I can muster, I sit back, slamming the chair into the floor. I hear a crack.

Some of the wood has given way.

I stand again, and then *BAM!* I sit back onto the chair. I feel it give in a little bit more.

Again and again I do this, until finally, with a shudder, creak, and then splintering sound, the chair disintegrates into a pile of wood beneath me. I land on my bottom, and the ropes around me immediately loosen, now that there is no chair frame to hold them taut.

I stand up, and the ropes that secured my torso to the chair fall off me and pool on the ground. My arms and legs are still tied, but at least I'm free from the chair.

I feel so clear headed. It occurs to me that though Ralph has tied my wrists together behind me, I can still move my fingers.

Kneeling, I maneuver my hands so that they are right above the ropes around my ankles. I slide the ankle-ropes around until my fingers feel the bulge of a knot. Within under a minute, I have the knot undone.

Next, I move my focus to the toolbox on the closet floor. It doesn't take me long to find what I'm looking for: a knife. I position it against the edge of the box, and then drag the remaining ropes over the blade.

The ropes give way, and my hands are freed. I immediately lift my hand to my face, and pull the tape off of my mouth.

Now, I just have to get through this door. I try the handle, but it doesn't turn. Ralph locked it.

I'm about to lift my foot to try a karate kick, when another thought strikes me.

"Reserare!" I say, mimicking the word I heard Azure mutter, when she wanted to unlock her apartment door.

The door flies open.

Wow! I could get used to this. Free from the closet, I move swiftly to my gun, which Ralph has left on a side table.

I feel like a million bucks as I run towards the cabin door, gun in one hand and handcuffs in my back pocket. Nothing can stop me now! I'm coming, Melanie!

It's darker outside then when I entered the cabin. The sun has settled behind one of the rocky peaks. In the dim lighting, I see Ralph's figure, sixty feet away. It looks like he has just barely managed to get Melanie into the rowboat, and is now turning to return to the cabin, for me.

I wish I could see his face, as he sees me running towards him, my hair flying.
I bet I'm a sight to behold.

I bet I look crazy. I think I'm smiling.

Yes. I'm definitely smiling.

Then I hear myself laugh.

Maybe I am crazy! That doesn't even bother me now.

As I run, I reach into my back pocket. My fingers close around the hard, curved steel of the handcuffs. I pull them out.

Ralph doesn't have a chance. When I reach him, I snap one cuff around one hand, and then quickly secure the other. I do all this single handedly. I feel like a superhero!

"What the --?" he sputters. "How did you -- where did you -- this is *impossible!*"

Everything that Chris told me is coming back to me now. I know that Ralph is still dangerous, even though he's handcuffed.

"On your knees!" I say, aiming the gun at him. My voice booms out with authority. Ralph does exactly as I say and sinks down to his knees.

I was right; his expression is priceless. I wish I had a camera. I could take a picture of this look of utter surprise on him and look at it when I need a confidence boost. The man can't believe that I've freed myself, and his shock is making him completely submissive. That *and* I have a gun pointed at him.

"Stay there!" I say. I keep the gun pointed at him as I walk backwards towards the boat.

"Melanie! Are you alright?" I ask, as I reach her.

I'm happy to see her eyes, though wide and full of fear, are bright with life. I set my gun down, within reach, and with half of my attention on the now whimpering Ralph and half on Melanie, I begin untying the ropes that bind her.

When I pull the tape off her mouth, she begins speaking softly. "Thank you -- oh, Penny, thank you, thank you!" She begins to weep.

I want to comfort her, but I have to keep a close eye on Ralph, so I resist. "It's okay," I say, as I return to my gun. My eyes are still on Ralph. "We're going to be okay," I repeat.

I aim the gun at Ralph, just so that he doesn't get any ideas.

What in the world am I going to do now? Send Melanie down the mountain for help? My mind begins turning over my options, but I'm interrupted by the sound of voices.

My eyes swivel to the place where the Rainbow Lake trail meets the clearing.

I see figures emerge.

"Penny? Penny!" I hear Chris call out.

"Over here!" I respond.

I see Chris clearly now. He's in his police uniform, and there's something in his arms.

Turkey?

Yes! He's holding my cat! Turkey must have run down the trail to get help!

There are two other officers just behind Chris, along with the Police Chief, Mayor Haywater, and Hiroku Itsu.

Hiroku is cradling Blueberry Muffin in her arms. I wave.

Blueberry gives a happy yip.

Chapter Sixteen

"They're just bruises," I say, as Chris takes the bag of melted ice from my hands. "I think I'll be fine."

"You should keep ice on it," Chris says, getting up from the couch. "I'll get you some more."

We're in his apartment, and I'm nestled onto his couch with a fleece blanket around me, and a cup of hot tea an arm's length away, on the coffee table.

Law and Order is playing on the television, and my belly is full of take out Chinese food.

"Could you get me my fortune cookie, while you're up?" I ask.

"What's the magic word?" Chris asks.

"Reserare" I whisper, under my breath. Then, louder, I say, "Please?"

Chris returns with a fresh bag of ice, and two cookies. He hands them to me. I set the bag of ice on the table, so that I can open my fortune cookie.

As I begin unwrapping it, he looks at me lovingly.

"What?" I ask.

"Nothing," he says. He sits back down on the couch and begins unwrapping his own cookie. "I'm just glad you're okay, that's all," he says, over the crinkling of plastic wrap.

"Me too," I say. "What do you think the Haywaters are doing right now?" I ask.

Chris thinks this over, and then says, "Having a good, long, honest discussion. It's about time, too."

I nod.

A few hours earlier, up at Trout lake, the police arrested Ralph. Cliff's happiness at finding his wife, safe and alive, was compromised when she tearfully began admitting her love for Joe.

"Cliff seemed so crushed when Melanie said she had been in love with Joe for years," I say.

"I don't blame him," Chris says, looking down at his unopened cookie. "Cliff and Melanie were married for over thirty years."

"At least she never cheated on him," I say. "She and Joe loved each other, but they never acted on it. Instead, they were going to wait until Melanie was divorced."

Melanie had admitted this, as well, when she'd made her tearful confession. Apparently, she had been waiting until Joe was no longer Cliff's employee before officially asking for a divorce so that she could confess her love to Joe.

"How do you think they booked their flights to Hawaii?" Chris asks.

"It must have all been done in secret," I say. "Each knew about the other's feelings. All it would have taken would be a few conversations. She'd mention the divorce, and her trip, and say that if Joe happened to be on the same flight, wouldn't it be great, or something like that."

"You've really thought this through," Chris says, raising a brow.

"I know, I know... I have a good imagination," I say, with a grin. "Do you think Cliff and Melanie will break up?"

Chris nods. "And it's for the best. If she doesn't love him, they shouldn't be together."

"It's so sad," I say. Then, before I can get too down about this, I crack open my fortune cookie. "Okay, let's see... I hope it's a good one. No!" I burst into a laugh as I read the one-word fortune on the little slip of paper within my cookie.

"It just says: Meh," I say.

"No way!" Chris says, laughing also. "That's all it says?"

"Yep." I place the slip of paper on my knee, and then pop one half of the cookie in my mouth. "What does yours say?" I ask, with my mouth full.

Chris opens his cookie. His face turns bright red.

"What is it?" I ask.

"Marriage will let you annoy one special person for the rest of your life," he reads aloud.

I burst out into laughter. Crumbs fly from my mouth. "You're kidding me!" I say, once I can speak. "It doesn't *really* say that, does it?"

"It does!" Chris starts laughing a little bit too. His laughter grows, until he's cracking up just as hard as I am.

By the time we stop, tears are streaming from the corner of my eyes. My abs and cheeks ache.

"That is too funny," I say, leaning forward and wiping my eyes. When I settle back onto the couch, I sink into the cushions, closer to Chris.

He scooches over, closer to me, and wraps his arm around my shoulder.

"Chris?" I say, as I curl up next to him.

"Hm?" he responds. He sounds as relaxed and happy as I feel.

"There's something I need to tell you."

"Anything, Penny," He says, giving me a little squeeze. "You can tell me anything."

"I've been... well, I'm reading a book. It's called the Art and Science of Becoming a Witch. Claudine Terra gave it to me."

"Oh yeah?" he says. "That's great."

"It's really changing my life. I think I'm -- no, I *know* I'm becoming a witch."

"A witch, hm?" Chris says.

"I can do all these things that I couldn't before," I say. "Like this evening, up at the lake. I was able to break free from the ropes and open the closet door, and I wasn't scared at all."

"You were really brave, Penny," he says, kissing the top of my head.

I sigh. Bravery doesn't even begin to describe what occurred at the cabin, but I'm too relaxed, happy, and exhausted to try to explain myself further.

"Don't forget about your ice," Chris says, reaching for the little plastic baggy of ice cubes.

I accept it and press it to my cheek.

Well. That went well. Very well. *Too* well. Chris has no clue what I really mean, when I say I'm becoming a witch.

But at least I told him.

It feels good.

I'm here, with Chris, and we're happy together. My cheeks are still sore from laughing.

"I like this," he says. "Just hanging out and laughing with you."

"Me too," I say, letting my head rest against his shoulder.

I'm filled with a feeling of content and happiness. Everything feels right, in this exact moment.

Which, I'm coming to understand, is all there is.

"Chris?" I say, softly.

"Yeah, Penny?" he responds.

"What if time really doesn't exist. What if it's just something that humans believe in, but it isn't real. Like what if there really isn't a past or a future, we just *think* there is."

Chris is quiet for a minute, and then he says. "You're weird."

I laugh a little. "Really, Chris," I say. "Something happened to me up at the cabin, in that closet. It was like time stopped being linear. There was only the exact moment that I was in -- nothing before it and nothing after it. I can't shake that feeling. I really like it."

I wait for Chris to respond. I can feel his breath, soft and warm against the top of my head. After a moment, he says, "I guess I don't really understand what you mean."

"What I mean is --" I bite my lip. Am I really going to do this? Yes. It feels right. "What I'm trying to say, Chris, is that I love you. Right now, in this moment, I love you."

I feel his lips kiss the top of my head. His warm, strong hand rubs my upper arm, up and down. "I love you too, Penny," he whispers. "I didn't want to tell you, because I thought you'd freak out. But I've loved you for a long, long time"

I nestle in closer to him. It feels so good to be held. A commercial comes on, and for a moment I zone out, watching little chocolate candies dance across the screen. The commercials end, and the show comes back on. Chris pulls me in closer, and I feel myself smile.

Chris didn't exactly take my confession of witchcraft seriously, but he didn't get upset, either. He doesn't understand what magic is, but is that really a problem? In this comfortable state that I'm in, in which the past and the future seem unreal, and now is the only moment that exists, I realize that it isn't a problem at all.

The next morning, I'm standing in Chris's apartment. I'm wearing one of his oversized tee shirts, and I'm mixing up waffle batter. Chris is standing at the coffee pot. It strikes me that the situation is almost exactly like the one I imagined, when I thought about telling Chris I was a witch.

I even need a measuring cup.

I know they're in the cupboard above Chris's head. Before I can give this another thought, my phone rings.

I reach for it, feeling relieved. What a timely interruption! Then I see that it's Cliff Haywater. For a minute, I feel a twinge of anxiety. Is he calling to yell at me for ruining his marriage? I reach for my necklace and give it a little squeeze. Warmth bursts through my chest, and my sense of calm returns.

I love the Power Spell!

I pick up the phone. "Hello?" I say, cheerfully.

"Hi, Penny? This is Cliff Haywater."

"Hi Cliff," I say. "What can I do for you?"

I hear Cliff clear his throat.

Chris reaches to the shelf filled with coffee mugs, and as he pulls one down, he holds it out towards me. He raises his brow and wiggles the cup.

I give a nod. I definitely want coffee.

As Cliff begins to speak, I turn away from Chris, so that I can give my full attention to the phone call.

"I wanted to thank you," Cliff says. "For all that you did last night. You showed a great deal of intelligence, courage, and valor."

"I don't know if I'd say valor," I say

"Well, I would," Cliff says. "You saved Melanie's life."

"How is Melanie doing?" I ask.

Again, Cliff clears his throat. "She's doing fine," he says. "She's happier, actually, than I've seen her in weeks. Last night we had quite a long talk. That's part of the reason I'm calling, actually."

"Oh?" I say.

"Melanie and I are parting ways," Cliff says. "We're going to remain friends, but our marriage is ending. Needless to say, I won't be using the plane tickets that I purchased yesterday morning."

"I'm sorry to hear that," I say. "But it sounds like it's for the best."

"It is," Cliff said. "I think we're both going to be happier. As for the two tickets that I bought -- I don't know if I told you this, but they're both non-refundable. And, seeing as you have been such a help to us, I wanted to see if…"

I hold my breath.

He continues. "If you wanted them. You could also have the hotel room that I booked," he says. "That will go to waste too, if no one uses it."

"Thank you!" I say.

"There's one more thing," he adds. "I want to give you a bonus. Two thousand dollars."

"Mayor Haywater, you don't have to do that."

"I know I don't *have* to, Penny. I *want* to. You risked your life last night, for Melanie. We're both beyond grateful. Words can't begin to express our gratitude. Neither can money, of course, but at least it's a start."

I'm speechless.

After a beat of silence, Cliff says, "I hope I haven't put you on the spot? You don't need to take the tickets, I just thought --"

"No!" I say. "I'll take them! Thank you, this is amazing!"

Cliff laughs.

"Thank *you*, Penny."

I hang up, grinning from ear to ear.

Two tickets to Hawaii! A hotel room! Two thousand dollars!

I know exactly who I'm going to give the other ticket to. I also know *exactly* what I'm going to do with the two thousand dollars.

Chapter Seventeen

"You're going to have to switch to the six millimeter circular needles now," Annie says, when I hold up the blue neckband I've been working on to show her my progress.

"Six millimeters," I say, as I set my knitting in my lap so that I can search through my carry-on suitcase, which is propped between my feet.

"I don't think I brought mine," I say.

"Don't worry, I have a pair you can use," Annie says.

As she reaches into her own carry-on bag, Marley and Cora approach us. Marley is carrying a plastic bag bursting with goodies.

"Who wants a snack?" Marley asks, in a sing song voice, as she sashays towards her waiting seat.

The Melrose airport is bustling with activity, but my friends stand apart from the crowd, due to their beachy attire. Marley is wearing a sleeveless pink blouse, printed with flamingos. Cora has a colorful sundress on. The tropical flowers splashed across it are hard to overlook.

Annie is also decked out in beach-ready clothing, thanks to the fact that Melanie generously allowed us to raid her closet for this trip.

I'm the only one who doesn't look ready to step off a plane into the Hawaiian airport. I wanted to wear all black. It's habit now, and plus, Hawaiian prints wouldn't go well with my new hand-painted cowboy boots. I'll change when we get there.

That's right -- my knitting circle is taking a field trip! In just a few moments, we're going to board a plane that will whisk us away to the sandy beaches of Oahu.

I used the bonus from Cliff to purchase two more tickets and a second hotel room, and now the four of us are in for the trip of a lifetime.

Marley has taken her seat, and is now passing bags of dried fruit, pretzels, and candy out to the rest of us. I hold onto Annie's package of chocolate covered raisins while she continues searching for knitting needles for me to use.

When she finds them, she uprights herself. "Here they are!" she says. "You know, just now as I was looking, I started to feel my satchel light up."

"You must have activated the Power Spell," I say, trading her the needles for the chocolates.

"I love it when that happens," Cora says. Instead of sitting, she's doing lunges in front of us, sipping her water bottle whenever she straightens her knee. Leave it to Cora to sneak in a bit of exercise while we wait for our flight.

"Me too," Marley says. "I wonder why yours is activating now, Annie?"

"Must be because my secret key ingredient is available," Annie says, with a pleased smile.

"Chocolate covered raisins?" I guess.

"Knitting needles?" guesses Cora.

Annie shakes her head.

We've been so busy preparing for the trip, over the past few days, that we've barely talked about our progress with the first cycle of ASBW. Now I wonder aloud, "Do you think that since it's called a *secret* ingredient, we have to keep it to ourselves?"

Marley shakes her head. "I don't think so. We're a coven. We're supposed to share things with each other, right?"

I think back to Azure's words about privacy. "Right," I say. "Annie, will you tell us, then? What's your secret key ingredient?"

Annie smiles even wider. "Good company," she says.

"Aww!" Marley says, throwing an arm over Annie's shoulder. "Thanks, Annie!"

"How about you?" I ask Marley. "Did you figure out yours?"

She nods. "I was outside of the van one night, washing dishes. You know how I set up that little portable water tank, and my folding table?"

I nod.

Cora laughs. "Don't you wish you had a kitchen sometimes?" she asks Marley.

"Don't *you* wish your kitchen ceiling was infinity feet tall, and sprinkled with stars?" Marley fires back. "I *have* a kitchen, Cora. It's the outdoors."

I prod Marley on. "What happened?" I ask.

"Well, I hooked my phone up to these little speakers that I have, and I started playing music. I was playing an album that my parents used to play, when I was little. It was one of those Best of Reggae compilations. One of my favorite songs came on and I was dancing and singing, and suddenly, this crazy feeling just washed over me."

"I know what you mean," I say. I've already told my friends about what happened to me, in the closet at the cabin. "It's hard to explain with words, isn't it?" I ask.

"Pretty much impossible," Marley says.

"So your secret ingredient is music?" Cora asks.

Marley nods. "I think it's one song, in particular. I was flooded with memories of being a child, and my mom and I dancing around the kitchen with that song playing. I remembered exactly what it felt like -- how I thought I could do anything in the world that I put my mind to."

"Maybe we can do anything we put our minds to, too," I say.

"I think we need to keep studying," Cora says. "We are only on cycle one. We have a lot to learn." She finishes her lunge, sips her water, and bounces over to the other leg.

"You're right," I say with a laugh. "What about you?" I ask Cora. "What's yours?"

"You're not going to believe this," Cora says.

"I'll believe anything, at this point," I say.

Cora smiles. "Order," she says. "I was rearranging my books according to spine height, and all of a sudden I had the feeling that you guys are talking about. It hit me so hard that I had to lie down flat on the living room floor, for about twenty minutes."

I nod. I'm reaching for the ball of yellow yarn, from my knitting bag, when a voice floats over the airport speakers. "Attention, guests. We will now begin boarding flight 657 to Oahu, Hawaii. We will begin boarding with our veterans, platinum ticket holders, and any guests that require extra assistance. Boarding group one can line up at the gate. Please have your boarding pass ready."

I glance down at the ticket at my side. "That's us!" I say. "We're boarding group one!"

Marley jumps to her feet, with a happy squeal. "Eeek!" she says. "I'm so excited!"

"Me too," Annie says.

Cora tucks her water bottle into her carry on, and then loops the bag's strap over her shoulder. "Penny, I think you should break up a marriage at least once a year. I could get used to this!" she says happily.

I roll my eyes.

Soon, we've boarded the plane and have settled into our seats. The four of us are lined up in a row, and each one of us has a knitting project on her lap. It's going to be a long flight, which means lots of knitting time.

And chatting.

The two go hand in hand, after all.

I'm at the window seat, next to me is Annie. I'm glad about this, because I expect to have many Icelandic sweater related questions over the next several hours. Cora is in the seat just past Annie, and Marley has the aisle seat.

Cora leans over Annie, so that she can see me. "Penny!" She says. "I almost forgot to ask you... how do you like your new neighbor?"

"Oh! Right. I can't believe we haven't talked about this!" I say, thinking of Azure. I should have told my coven sisters about the new witch in town long ago. There has just been so much going on.

"I know!" Cora says, looking strangely pleased. She wiggles her eyebrows. "I don't think it's a coincidence," she says.

"I don't even believe in coincidences anymore," I say, not quite sure why Cora is acting so coy. "And this definitely isn't one. Azure said that she moved in part time so that she could help us protect the portal, if we need it. But, now that we've done the Power Spell, I don't think we'll --"

"Wait, *Azure?* I'm not talking about Azure," Cora says.

Now I'm confused. "But she's my new neighbor," I say. "She moved into Unit B."

An announcement starts playing over the plane speakers, and Cora and I pause our discussion while it blares out safety instructions. Cora leans back, and I look out the window, at the paved tarmac below. Airport workers in bright yellow vests are wheeling suitcases into the luggage compartment.

Finally, the long-winded instructions come to an end. Cora pops forward again.

"Azure moved into Unit B?" Cora says.

"Yes. I should have told you all earlier. She said that she's been watching us, and is concerned that the portal is vulnerable because we're so unskilled. I wonder if she saw how well we did with the Power Spell though!"

"She's the leader of the air coven, is that right?" Annie asks, as her fingers work steadily on her knits and purls. "Not the nicest young lady, if I remember correctly."

"Who were *you* talking about?" I ask Cora. I'm too distracted to answer Annie's question just now. "Do I have *another* new neighbor?"

"You do," Cora says mysteriously.

"Well, tell me!"

"First, tell us how it's going with Chris. You two seemed pretty lovey-dovey when he dropped us off at the airport! And he and your cat seem to be good friends now, too."

I laugh. "I think Turkey would move into Chris's apartment, if that was an option. Turkey loves the guy. Ever since that night at the cabin--"

"Turkey ran down the trail, to get Chris?" Annie says, as her needles click.

I nod.

Marley, from her position at the end of the row, leans forward. "You have one smart cat, Penny. I think we all knew that already."

"He heard me cry out and was worried about me, and he thought I might need help. He ran all the way back down the trail, into town. Straight to the police station -- with Blueberry Muffin at his heels."

"You mean Cora's boss's Chihuahua?" Annie asks.

I smile. "Yup. Turns out precious little Blueberry is a little heartier than her owner was giving her credit for. Turkey said that she enjoyed the run!"

Cora laughs. "I think Hiroku is going to let Blueberry out of the carrier more often now," she says. She's working on a hat she's just started. So far, it looks alot like the neckline of my sweater: a knitted circular loop.

There's a lull in our conversation. The passengers that boarded the plane after us have found seats, and now the plane is starting to roll down the runway. The captain announces that we are getting into position for takeoff.

As the plane begins to pick up speed, I return to Cora's first question. "Chris and I are doing great," I say. "This is actually the happiest I've felt with our relationship in a long time. We're in a really good place."

"They say 'I love you' now," Marley informs my friends.

Cora and Annie *oooh* and *ahhh* over this for a minute, while I continue to blush.

"I don't get it," I say, once my friends have had their fun. "What does that have to do with my new neighbor?"

Cora talks while she knits. "Well, the last time I talked to you about Chris, you'd just had an argument with him. I thought things weren't going well, and I thought if you were going to enter the dating scene again, then you might be interested to know that --" She stops short, as the plane's wheels leave the ground.

There's a humming sound as they are retracted into the engine. The plane angles upwards.

Cora releases her knitting and grips her arm rests. "Sorry -- my stomach always flips at this part," she says.

"I *love* this part," I say.

"As I was saying," Cora continues, while still gripping her arm rest, "If you were to enter the dating scene again, you might be interested to know that *Max* is going to be your new neighbor. He's moving into Blackbear apartments, Unit D. Hiroku helped him sign the lease."

For the next few minutes, as the plane climbs higher and higher into the sky, I try to process what Cora has just shared.

Doctor Max Shire is going to be my neighbor.

At first, I get a kind of queasy, nervous-and-excited-at-the-same-time feeling. It hits my gut, and then my chest.

If Max is going to be my neighbor, I'll be seeing him quite a bit. How will I handle being around him, now that I've entered into a more serious relationship with Chris?

My thoughts start to spin out of control.

But then, I look out the plane window, just at the plane pierces through a thick layer of clouds.

We've reached clear skies. The plane levels out. Below us, a carpet of puffy, light clouds spread out like an ocean.

My life is full of uncertainties. They stretch out in every direction, as far as the eye can see, just like the clouds below me. Will I stay with Chris? Will I be successful in my PI business? Will Hiroku fire me from the nannying gig? Will I fall for Max? Is it truly my destiny to be a witch?

I don't have all the answers.

I don't know if I *want* to have all the answers.

As long as I can get to this place -- above the clouds -- I know I'll be okay.

I close my eyes and hear the words I've come to know and love, float through my mind.

Your place of power is above the clouds.

I take a deep breath, and then open my eyes.

The speaker above my seat clicks on. "Ladies and gentlemen," the captain says. "I'm happy to announce we've reached our cruising altitude of thirty-five thousand feet. I invite you to sit back and enjoy the flight as we make our way to sunny Oahu."

The announcement ends, and Marley gives a little whoop.

I join her, and then say happily, "Hawaii, here we come!"

The End

Dear Reader,

Thank you for diving into the fictional world of Hillcrest with me! I love writing about Penny and her coven of witch sisters. I hope that you enjoy reading about their magical adventures.

Have you read the prequel to this series? I offer it for free to all readers (Find it here: BookHip.com/NATZXF). Learn all about how Penny inherited her copy of ASBW. You'll also witness Penny and Turkey's first telepathic communication (hint -- Turkey is *not* a fan of Penny's singing!).

You can also check out other books in the series,
#1 The Case of the Power Spell
#2 The Case of the Banishing Spell
#3 The Case of the Desire Spell
#4 The Case of the Trust Spell
#5 The Case of the Vision Spell
#6 The Case of the Voice Spell
#7 The Case of the Earth Spell

I would love to hear from you. Send along an email (amorette@amoretteanderson.com) and I'll be sure to respond!

Thank you again for reading. I am so grateful.

Amorette

Made in the USA
Columbia, SC
13 September 2021